A Faerie Tale Romance Novella

THE WOLF GATE

a Retelling of Little Red Riding Hood

by

HANNA SANDVIG

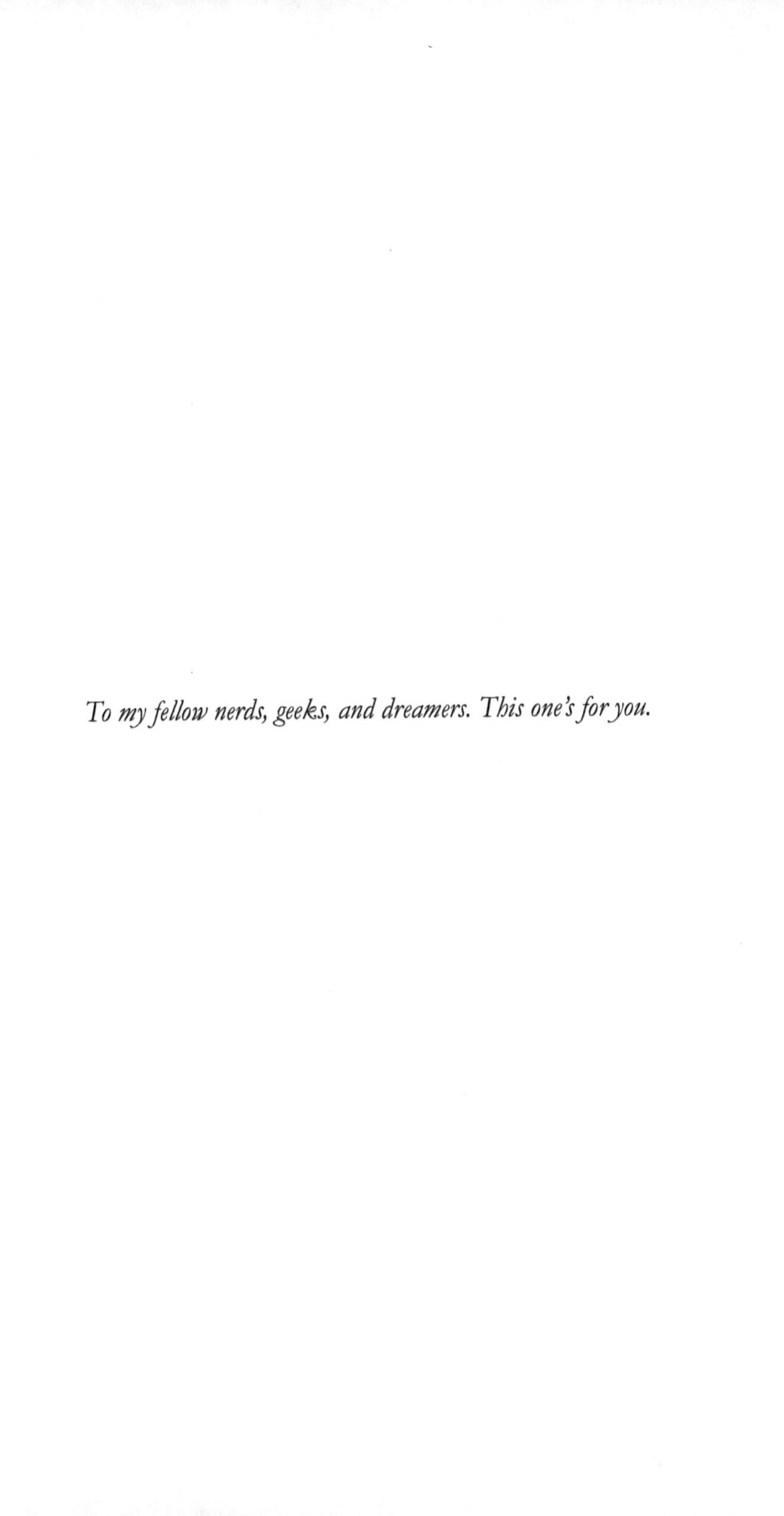

To my fellow nerds, geeks, and dreamers. This one's for you.

TÍR NA NÓG
N
W E
S
Liadan's Tower
the Dwarven Kingdom
the Unseelie Court
Bronach's Cabin
Bhanmhor Sliabhraon
Kilinaire Castle
Inner Sea
the Elder Fae
the Isle of Mist
Port Delfare
Southern Grasslands
the Seelie Court

Chapter 1

"That's it." Neve pulled my cup away from me and hid it behind the bar. "You're cut off."

"Nooooo," I whimpered. "Sweet, sweet nectar, come back to me!"

"Audrey, you've had three cups of coffee. It's eight already. In the evening. You'll be up all night and sending me ridiculous texts at two-thirty in the morning."

"I would never." I gave my best friend my most tragic puppy-dog eyes.

"That's what you said last week." Neve held up her phone.

I pushed my dark-framed glasses up on my nose and examined the screen. It read: *Still can't sleep. Never let me drink coffee again. If you see me drinking coffee, slap it out of my hand. 2:36AM.*

"I was clearly delirious." I leaned back on my barstool. "You've gotten cold in your old age."

"Delirious from sleep deprivation! And if I'm old at seventeen, you must be ancient at eighteen. I'm the picture of youth." Neve pulled open the retro pink fridge behind the bar and peered inside.

"And yet, so heartless."

"Shhh. Have some pie. It's apple ginger." She slid a slice of pie across the polished wood on a floral china plate.

Pie in the Sky, Pilot Bay's finest cafe (okay, only cafe, unless you counted the coffee counter at the gas station), was owned by Neve's parents. Her dad handled the money, and her mom was responsible for the pretty, shabby-chic decor, but everyone knew that it was Neve who was the genius with pastries. Her chocolate cookies could bring boys to their knees.

When you added that to her curvy, tattooed, vintage pin-up-girl vibe, she was irresistible. Not that she seemed to care. She said the local boys lacked a certain something. Her aloof attitude only made them love her more.

I, on the other hand, couldn't even get my boyfriend to meet me for coffee.

"I have to close in fifteen minutes. Did Dylan text you back? Is he coming?" My friend pulled out a bandana from her apron pocket and tied her dark hair back. Cleaning mode engaged.

"Nothing. I even promised him free pie." I took a bite of my own pie. So flaky. So perfect.

"Humph, I'm not sure he's worthy of apple ginger." Neve grabbed a cloth and scrubbed the counter aggressively. "I'm sorry. I know you like him. I'm just not sure why."

"Well…it isn't for his punctuality. You do have to admit he's pretty to look at." When he was around. "And the accent is nice."

"Gavin also had that lovely Irish accent, and he was never late." Neve picked up my plate and wiped under it before setting it back down.

"Could we please not talk about my ex-boyfriend? Like…ever?" I took another bite and considered telling Neve the real reason I had asked Dylan to meet me tonight. But while I was still chewing, the cafe's phone rang.

"Hi, Aunt Chloe." Neve tucked the phone between her ear and shoulder and kept cleaning. "Uh huh. I have two chocolate with salted caramel buttercream and six vanilla bean with lavender buttercream." She laughed. "Of course, chocolate always sells better. I can't get away for another hour, though. I still have to clean up and cash out."

I listened with half my attention while finishing my pie and composing a scathing text to my absent boyfriend.

"Oh, yes, she's here. How did you guess?"

I looked up at Neve in surprise. Although maybe I shouldn't have been. Her Aunt Chloe knew everything. No story too big, no gossip too small.

"I'll ask her, just a sec." Neve pulled the phone from her ear. "Audrey, I know you're waiting for Dylan, but would you mind making a delivery for me? Aunt Chloe needs some cupcakes. She's expecting her book club ladies and the one in charge of snacks is sick. It's a dessert emergency."

I glared at my phone and hit send with a sigh. "Fine. If he happens to stop by, tell him I went home. I assume his phone must have gotten run over by a car, or he'd be answering my texts."

"What if Dylan got run over by the car?" Neve moved the glass cover from the cake stand to the counter and carefully boxed her tasty creations.

"Then, I will consider forgiving him." I tucked my phone into my backpack and accepted the pink pastry box from my friend.

"Thank you, Audrey. Come over in the morning and we'll re-dye the ends of your hair, I can barely see the pink anymore."

"Sure, sure." I slid off my stool. Anything to make my pale, freckly blonde self more interesting. Reaching across the bar, I hugged my friend. "Thanks for the pie. See you tomorrow."

The rain I ran through earlier today had stopped, but the sidewalk was still wet and the air felt cool for July. I dodged puddles the size of small lakes as I walked down Main Street on my way to Miss Chloe's house. Yes, Pilot Bay had only one major road through town, and yes, it's called Main Street. You had to give the town fathers props for clarity if not originality.

You might have thought that at eighteen I could probably drop the Miss, but sadly, that's impossible. Miss Chloe was Pilot Bay's head librarian, and she'd been shushing me and my friends since we were toddlers.

Miss Chloe was not actually Neve's aunt. They weren't even related. She was more like a godmother if anything, but the Klassens weren't Catholic, so aunt it was.

I cut across the street and past the mishmash of houses—mansions to trailers—on the west end of town, before coming to the dirt road leading to Miss Chloe's house. She lived just beyond the outskirts of town, but the road was pretty, lined with tall pine trees and mossy rocks. It was just starting to get dark out, but I didn't think I'd have any trouble making it home before night fell.

I turned the last bend in the road and there was Miss Chloe's house. It looked like a fairy-tale cottage, with a tall peaked roof. Climbing roses covered the shingled siding around one corner. The windows glowed in the dusky evening light.

I climbed the front steps and knocked on the bright red front door. Instead of the usual lion, her brass knocker was shaped like a bear's head. More appropriate for British Columbia, I supposed.

Miss Chloe poked her curly gray head out the door and smiled when she saw me.

"Audrey, you've saved me. None of the book club ladies were going to get to the bakery in time." She adjusted her gold-rimmed glasses and stepped back into the house. "Come in for a minute. I have something for you to take to Neve."

"Oh, I don't know how much the cupcakes cost," I protested. "I'm just the delivery girl."

"No, no, it's not about money." Miss Chloe waved me in, and I obediently entered. I'd walked over here with Neve before, but I'd never been inside. The entryway was spotless. A gilded mirror hung on the wall, flanked by paintings of roses.

"You'll be seeing her tomorrow, right?" she asked. "For the anime festival in Rossland?"

"Um, yes? I don't know if I'd actually call it a festival." I tugged at the hem of my black Naruto t-shirt. "I'm not sure more than five people in the Kootenays even watch anime. I don't have high hopes."

Miss Chloe just smiled and opened the box of cupcakes, inhaling deeply. "It's going to take all my willpower to wait until the other ladies arrive," she said happily. "Neve's baking improves every day."

I nodded politely, trying not to look too anxious to leave. I didn't actually want to walk home through the woods in the dark.

The older lady shut the pastry box with a sigh and headed into the house. "I'll just find that item for you. Come sit in the living room. Don't worry about your shoes."

I padded after her, having already slipped out of my red chucks. Canadian force of habit. The living room smelled of roses with giant bouquets gracing the mantle and coffee table.

"You sure like roses." I held my backpack on my lap and perched on the edge of the plush couch. It was heaped with pillows which all had—surprise!—embroidered roses on them. Except one. I picked it up, squinting at the beautifully stitched design. Was that Iron Man?

"They're terribly friendly flowers, you know." Miss Chloe opened a wooden chest under the window and rummaged around. "I know it's in here somewhere…"

"I really should be going soon." I looked past her, out the window where the forest was growing darker. "The fastest way home is the trail through the forest, but it—"

"It's getting dark. Yes dear, I know. Ah, here it is." Miss Chloe pulled a long swath of red velvet from the blanket box. She shook it out with an air of satisfaction, and I leaned forward, embroidered Iron Man forgotten, as I saw what she held.

CHAPTER 2

THE CLOAK WAS GORGEOUS, WITH A deep hood and thick folds of scarlet velvet that would fall nearly to the ground if I wore it. Gold thread embroidered the edges in curling, twining designs. A pair of heavy-looking gold clasps held the front together.

Miss Chloe plopped it in my lap, and I found myself petting the plush red fabric. It felt so cozy, and…was it buzzing somehow? I squinted at the embroidery. The golden knotwork pattern seemed to spin in an intricate twisting pattern, growing in depth like fractals around the threads. I shook my head and the glowing pattern faded.

Well, that was weird. Neve had been right to cut off my caffeine. I obviously needed an early bedtime tonight. I folded the cloak up as well as I could before cramming it into my backpack.

"You'd best be heading home." Miss Chloe peered out the window. Daylight was fading quickly now.

I stood, swinging my backpack onto my shoulder with a grunt. The cloak felt heavier than I expected. "What does Neve need a cloak for anyway?"

"Oh, you never know when it might come in handy," Miss Chloe called back over her shoulder as I followed her to the door. She stopped abruptly in the entryway, and I almost ran into her. "Audrey." She examined me through her gold-framed glasses. "I regret not being able to give you more attention."

"Um, that's okay." I had no idea what the librarian was apologizing for. When had she ignored me? "I don't really read all that much."

"You'll do well." She gave my shoulder a reassuring pat. "You're stronger than you realize."

"Thanks?" Should I tell Neve that her aunt was possibly struggling with dementia? "I really should go now, though."

Miss Chloe opened the door and stepped out onto the porch. She glanced up at the sky, purple and cloudy in the twilight. "Good luck, my dear."

"It's only a fifteen-minute walk to my house, Miss Chloe," I said with a laugh as I ran down the stairs. "I'll be fine. Enjoy your book club." I definitely needed to check in with Neve about her.

Pilot Bay was nestled into the mountains with Kootenay Lake on one side and forests surrounding the rest of town. There were trails all around the edges of the community, some leading into the mountains, some creating shortcuts to other neighborhoods. I'd grown up here and I knew the trails as well as the true roads in the area. Halfway back to town from Miss Chloe's, I turned onto a bike trail that would connect to the little path running past my backyard.

It was darker on the smaller trail, with the trees thick around me, but it would take twice as long to walk through town. So, I walked quickly and tried to keep my eyes on the path instead of scanning the trees for the reflective gleam of cougar eyes. No one had seen a cougar around town. This year.

I found the crossroads with no problem and started down the little path to home. It was almost full dark now, but I wasn't worried.

Not until I heard the howl.

I stopped in my tracks. I'd always heard about wolves living in our mountains, but I'd thought I'd have to be lucky to see one, they were so rare. My pulse kicked up at the wolf's howl, but it sounded far away, deep in the woods. For a moment, I listened to the winds whisper through the trees. With a shiver, I started moving again. I'd have to tell Neve I heard a wolf. It'd be a good story.

Then I heard an answering howl and all the hair stood up on my arms. This one was *not* far away. I broke into a jog, scanning the trees, not in the least bit prepared when a large gray wolf bounded onto the path in front of me.

I shrieked, my heart hammering.

Its pale, yellow eyes bore into me. I froze. I couldn't even breathe. Now I could say I'd seen a wolf. I did not feel lucky.

I pivoted in a spray of dirt and bolted from the path into the forest.

This might not have been the wisest move. In my panic, I thought I could hide in the dark forest, but the thing was, the wolves could see in the dark.

And I couldn't.

I crashed along blindly through the undergrowth, my legs getting battered and scraped by unseen branches, the wolf right on my heels. Then I heard a second howl.

Seriously, though? Weren't wolves supposed to be more afraid of me than I was of them?

With a crash and a snarl, a second, darker, wolf caught up to the first and nearly ran it over in its eagerness to eat me first. I tripped in the dark, foolishly focusing on wolves instead of my feet.

The wolves untangled themselves. Two pairs of gleaming eyes watched me climb to my feet.

"N-nice wolves." I held up my hands. "Please don't eat me."

One stepped closer, growling, but the dark wolf lunged for me, snapping at my ankles. I took off through the forest again, even though I knew I would never be able to outrun them.

In fact, I hardly took more than a few steps when one of the wolves crashed into me from the side. I fell beneath its weight. This was going to be the end for me. No more Audrey.

But I was surprised by three things. One, it was suddenly bright out, as bright as midday. Two, instead of falling into a bush, I landed in a snowbank. A snowbank in July. But most surprising of all was the third thing. The heavy weight that pushed me into the snowbank, was not, in fact, a wolf. It was Gavin McKenna, my ex-boyfriend.

Given a choice, I might have chosen the wolf.

CHAPTER 3

SIX MONTHS AGO, WE'D BEEN PRETENDING to pay attention in History (all except Isobel Watson who sat beside me with a Richelle Mead novel tucked discreetly into her textbook), when the principal interrupted our class to introduce two exchange students from Ireland.

Now, looking back, there were some warning signs. Both of them were over six feet tall, and not tall in that gangly way like all the other boys in grade twelve. These two were filled out. Shoulders, forearms, the whole thing. Perfect skin, perfect teeth. They were clearly too good to be true. And did I mention the accents? I was a sucker for an Irish accent. Me and every other girl in North America.

Dylan was plenty good looking, if you went for the whole blond, blue-eyed, football star look. But Gavin. Well, Gavin looked like trouble. Green eyes, dark hair with a messy, careless curl to it. One tan arm was covered in dark blue tattoos swirling up from his wrist and disappearing under the edge of his t-shirt. At first, I thought he had earrings, but on closer inspection (and yes, he warranted a closer inspection), the glints of gold were actually plugs. Not giant, ear-distending plugs, but just big enough to be…interesting.

The principal droned on, but Gavin turned his head and caught me looking. He gave me a lazy smile. A wiser girl would have looked away (or, like Isobel, continued to read with no apparent interest in what was going on). But I couldn't help myself.

I smiled back.

Once we'd untangled ourselves from the snowbank, I did what any reasonable girl would do, given the circumstances. I slapped my ex-boyfriend across the face.

Gavin staggered back, those pretty green eyes asking me what he had done to deserve such treatment.

So many things.

I struggled to my feet in the knee-deep snow. My canvas runners were full of snow, and I regretted my choice in wearing shorts today.

Gavin glared at me while he brushed snow off his gray t-shirt and dark jeans. While he recovered, I used the moment of peace to take a look around.

We weren't in Kansas anymore. Not only was it daytime and snowy, but we were high up in the mountains. Towering rocky peaks surrounded the icy ridge line we stood on, the wind whipping sparkling crystals of snow around us in swirls. I could see green forests below, the trees growing shorter and twistier as they crept up the mountain, but it was bare of life up this high. Just rock, snow, and my least favorite person.

"Where are we?" I demanded. "What did you do?"

"What makes you think *I* did anything?"

Ugh, that stupid, sexy accent.

Gavin shook the snow out of his dark hair. The ends curled from the dampness. Dumb gorgeous hair. His gold plugs glinted in his ears.

"Well, did you?" I asked.

"Possibly."

"Undo it! I'm freezing."

"That's all you have to say? You're suddenly transported to a breathtaking mountain range and you're not even curious about what happened?"

"I'm too cold to be curious." I rubbed my bare arms but it didn't make me feel any warmer. I glared at Gavin's arms. They were as impressive as ever, well-muscled with dark blue Celtic knots and swirls covering the left one. What they didn't have were goosebumps. "Take me home and I'll ask you all the questions you like. In a million years or so. When I'm speaking to you again." The bite in my words was undercut by my chattering teeth.

"I can't."

"What?!"

"You can't go back yet. That other wolf will be right there, looking for you."

"What do you mean, other wolf? You're talking as if you're one of the wolves."

Gavin gave me a courtly bow. No, this was ridiculous. I must be delirious from the cold. But then-…shouldn't the cold be part of the hallucination? I was, for real, losing feeling in my fingers.

"You see..." Gavin began.

"Wait a sec." I pulled my backpack off and tugged the zipper open.

"Audrey, could you please focus?" His voice rose.

"Can't focus, too busy freezing." I pulled out the yards of red velvet from my pack. I gave the cloak a shake and swirled it onto my shoulders. The cool satin lining warmed against my skin as I tugged the deep hood up, blocking out the wind. Much better. I hoped the velvet wouldn't get damaged by the snow. It was so cold that the snow felt dry, but I wanted to deliver it to Neve in decent condition.

My numb fingers fumbled with the gold clasp. Suddenly, Gavin stood in front of me, fastening the closure.

"Where did you get this cloak?" His fingers felt warm as they brushed against mine. I slapped them away.

"None of your business. Let's get back to you. You were implying that you're a wolf, which is clearly ridiculous. I only date humans."

Gavin let out a bark of laughter.

"Fine, then." I rolled my eyes. "Show me your furry side."

"I'm only a wolf at night. It's a curse. Much like my incredible good looks."

"You poor thing. If I keep rolling my eyes, I'm going to get dizzy. You're trying to tell me that you're a wolf by night, and a human by day? Like a werewolf?"

"Fae."

"Pardon?"

"Wolf by night, fae by day."

"Come again?"

Gavin took hold of my shoulders and spun me around. We now faced a stone arch. It looked like a doorway, with carved columns and stones with swirling patterns etched into them. Yet it led to nothing but more drifting snow. Two gold plates were bolted to the columns. Strange. Who would build a structure like that out here in the middle of nowhere?

"It's a faerie gate," Gavin said, right by my ear. "We went through a gate in the forest near Pilot Bay and traveled to Faerie. We're standing on the *Bhanmhor Sli-abhraon*, the mountain range dividing the seelie and unseelie lands in *Tír na nÓg*."

My mind scrambled to catch up. Gavin's explanation was crazy. But was there any sane explanation for suddenly being transported onto a frozen mountaintop?

"We're in...a fairyland?"

"Faerie. Yes."

"And you're a fairy?"

"Yes."

I turned on frozen feet and gave him a long look. "But with less wings and more fur?"

"Pretty much."

I raised an eyebrow.

"So untrusting," he sighed. He reached up and, with a faint grimace, popped one of his plugs out of its earlobe.

My jaw dropped. Gavin's normal, human ear stretched up to a sharp point. He did the same with his other ear, and it too changed shape. Something about his face shifted as well. He was still Gavin, but...sharper. Even better-looking than before, but I would take that sentiment to my grave.

"Um." That was all I could come up with. Really, what could you say?

Gavin smirked, slipping the gold plugs into his jeans pocket. Still obnoxiously cocky, no matter what shape his ears were.

"Right." I backed up slowly toward the stone arch. "This has been…interesting, but I'm going to go home now."

Gavin lunged forward, grabbing my arm. "Haven't you been listening to anything I said? It's not safe. Just wait a minute."

"I try to ignore as much of what comes out of your mouth as possible." I shook my arm free. "Why will it be safe in a minute?"

"Well, more like an hour or two. Time flows differently in Faerie, usually much faster. An hour here is only minutes in your world."

"An hour or two?" I lifted a snow-covered sneaker. "You know I'm wearing shorts, yes? How are you not freezing?"

"I run hot. Want a piggyback?"

I let my eyes answer for me. My pointy-eared ex opened his mouth to say something when his eyes widened in alarm.

"Get down." His hand on my shoulder shoved me into the snow.

"Are you crazy?" I spat snow out of my mouth and struggled to rise, but he kept his hand on my shoulder as he crouched beside me.

"I need you to be perfectly quiet. Think snowy thoughts. He can't find you here." There was real fear in Gavin's voice. He spread the cloak out to cover me and stood.

"Think snowy thoughts?" I grumbled under my breath. I couldn't feel my feet. Snowy thoughts weren't a problem, but I didn't see what good they would do me. My glasses fogged up as I huddled under my cloak. I considered standing, but Gavin seemed honestly worried. What could stalk us on a magical mountain top? Giant polar bear? Yeti?

"Gavin!" another Irish accent called out.

My boyfriend?

Why was I hiding from Dylan? Was Gavin finally feeling jealous? Why should I freeze in a snowbank just because my ex had issues? But then...what was Dylan doing here? Clearly these boys were not actually from Ireland.

"Dylan," Gavin said evenly. I saw them facing off in my mind. Dark versus blond. Both too tall and too broad-shouldered to pass for an average high school boy. I really should have known something was up with them.

"It took me a bit to figure out where you'd gone. I didn't realize there was a gate on that end of town."

"Me neither," Gavin lied smoothly. "Fell through by accident. We should head back. Kylian wants us all over by the Rose Gate tonight. The Queen has warned him to keep that bookish girl, Isobel, away from the gate."

"Right, right." Dylan's voice sounded relaxed. "Where's the girl?"

The girl? I was the girl? I mean, we weren't exactly soul mates, but we'd been dating for five weeks. I was pretty sure he knew my name. I was about to stand up and give him a piece of my mind when something clicked. Dylan must be the second wolf. I shivered. And not just from the cold. I needed to seriously reevaluate my taste in boys. I stayed crouched in the snow. It was probably smart to listen a bit more.

"Isobel Watson?"

"Of course not. My sweet little girlfriend."

"She must be back in the forest still. Why were you chasing her anyway? You don't think she's the lost princess?"

"Audrey?" Dylan laughed. "No. She's cute enough. And decent in bed. But she's not exactly princess material."

Wait, what?! That boy hadn't gotten so much as a hand up my shirt. What was he trying to do?

"I was just having a bit of fun, is all," he continued. I heard the crunch of footsteps come closer. "You know how I love to hunt. But if you say she's not here, she's not here."

I held perfectly still as Dylan walked around me. How did he not see me in my bright red cloak?

"If the girl was around, she probably would have come right over to me when I showed up. She's prettier than she is smart."

I gave a small, involuntary gasp of pure rage. Not very smart? Not very smart?! This from a boy who couldn't even install an app on his phone without my help, let alone create one?

The footsteps stopped.

I held my breath.

"Well, hello, little girl."

CHAPTER 4

I SCRAMBLED TO MY FEET, BUT IT WAS TOO late. Dylan stood right beside me.

He grabbed the back of my hood, fisting through the velvet to hold my hair in an iron grip. I gasped in shock. Dylan had never been much fun, but I'd just thought he was boring. I'd never expected him to be cruel.

"Little girl?! My name is *Audrey*!" I kicked back and hit him square in the knee. He grunted but didn't let go. "And we are *through*!"

The blond jerk spun me around to face him, holding my arm painfully tight. I shuddered. This had been lurking under his casual smiles all along? How he must have been laughing at me the entire time we'd been together.

"Dallying with a human girl in Faerie when we have a mission in the human world?" His eyes never left mine. He licked his lower lip. "It's not the smartest idea, but I could be convinced to join in."

White hot rage flooded me. I tried to pull back and aim my next kick a little higher, but I was interrupted by a fist flying past my ear, right into Dylan's face. As he tumbled back into the snowbank, Gavin grabbed my hand and pulled me to a run.

"Let go of me! I can't kill him if I'm running away." I stumbled through the knee-deep snow on frozen feet.

"Will you just listen to me for once!" Gavin resisted my attempts to tug my hand free and ran faster than I would have thought possible, hauling me along the rough path behind him. "You can't take him on, he's the pack alpha for a reason. I'm not even sure I can take him, certainly not while protecting you. Come on."

I glanced behind. Dylan was only a few feet behind us, cursing and clutching a bleeding nose while he ran. I looked back at Gavin and stopped in my tracks for a moment when I saw what we were running toward, before his momentum yanked me forward again.

"Stop!"

"Just trust me on this."

"But. Cliff!"

Gavin didn't slow down. He gripped my hand more tightly and leapt off the snowy cliff, forcing me to half stumble, half jump after him.

I screamed as we plummeted past the rocky cliff face, the wind whipping my hair. Gavin pulled me to him and rolled as we hit the snowbank below. I gasped for breath, but he was already up, hauling me to my frozen feet.

"Glasses!" I yanked my arm free and felt around me in the powdery snow.

"Just leave them." Gavin looked up anxiously.

I threw my best glare in the general direction of his blurry silhouette and ran my frozen fingers over the snow until they closed around the cold plastic of my frames.

"So dramatic," Dylan's voice drifted down. I shook the snow off my glasses and slid them on to see him peering down at us from the top of the cliff. "As fun as you made that look, I'd better go let The Huntsman know you'll be late. He's going to be very interested in all of this. I'm taking care of the gate, so you two just sit tight." He gave us a cheery wave with one hand, the other one still holding his bloody nose. "See you soon, little girl."

"I hate you!" I shouted. It wasn't the snappiest comeback, but truer words had never been spoken.

My boyfriend—my ex-boyfriend—just waved again and tromped out of sight toward the stone arch.

I turned back to my ex-ex-boyfriend. Okay, this was ridiculous. I clearly couldn't be trusted to date ever again.

"What now, genius?" I waved at the cliff. "How are we getting back up? Do your werewolf powers include rock climbing? Levitation, perhaps?"

"We're not going back up." Gavin peered into the forest below us.

"But…up is where the gate is. How will we get home if we don't go up? If I die out here—"

"Will you just be quiet and listen to me for once!" bellowed Gavin.

"Um—"

"I'm trying to keep you alive. I wish I knew why I'm even bothering."

"Hey!"

"You can't go back through that gate. Dylan will have sealed it here and in Pilot Bay. Your charming lover doesn't want to risk any pack members wandering be-tween realms without his supervision, and only the Hunts-man and the pack alpha can lock and unlock the gates. I can't."

"Ex-lover," I interjected, pulling my glasses back off to dry them on my t-shirt. "Well, technically…"

"He's dangerous," Gavin said more softly. "Surely you can see that by now. We can't risk checking the gate, and we can't stay here and wait for him. He doesn't have to pretend to be nice anymore, not now that you know what he truly is."

"A lying wolf, you mean?" I flung back at him. Gavin winced.

"Exactly." He avoided looking me in the eyes. "Now come on, we need to get inside before night falls." He started walking down the mountainside at an angle.

"Inside where?"

He didn't look back, just kept on walking. I sighed and trudged after him, trying to step in his footsteps in the deep snow. His stride was much longer than mine, and even longer when he was in a snit.

"Does inside come with wool socks?" I asked plaintively as I missed a footprint and lost my leg from the knee down into the powdery snow. "What about hot cocoa? Oooh, is there magic hot cocoa?"

No response. I quickened my pace, not wanting to be left behind on the frozen mountain top.

It didn't take long for the adrenaline from our encounter with Dylan to wear off, leaving me with nothing but numb legs and regrets. I couldn't really feel my feet anymore, which surely wasn't good, and even though I was wrapped in the velvet cloak, my hands still froze. Also, my nose. And had I mentioned my legs? How had I gotten myself into this mess?

If I'd never met these stupid boys, I would be home on my cozy couch watching season fourteen of

Bleach and texting Neve. Past Audrey had made some stupid decisions, that was for sure.

38

Chapter 5

For a month after the "Irish exchange students" joined my History class, I walked around in a state of constant Gavin awareness. He was in two of my four classes. History, of course, where he charmed us all with his cluelessness about North American colonization (and, in retrospect, human history in general), and Physical Education, where he charmed us all with his ridiculous physique.

Oh yes, I was not the only one pretending to ignore the tattooed boy with the unruly dark hair, while watching his every move.

But I was the only one he watched back.

At first, I was sure it was my imagination. I wasn't someone who got a lot of attention from boys. I wasn't sporty, or social, or hair flippy, or whatever it is guys usually went for. I once overheard one of the boys in my grade describe me as "kind of pretty, but weird" and that was probably as good a description as any. And there were plenty of girls who were more than kind of pretty, and not weird.

But the more time passed, the more I became sure he was just as aware of me as I was of him. I could feel his eyes following me whenever we were in the same room, although he never really hung out with anyone but Dylan. Usually he looked away, casually, as soon as I turned, but once he gave me a slow wink that I was sure had turned my whole face as pink as the ends of my hair.

Neve teased me relentlessly about it. She was in grade eleven, so we didn't have any of the same classes, but we always spent lunch hour together. I'd work on whatever app I was coding, and Neve would try to fatten me up with whatever her newest creation was.

"You should ask him out," she told me during one such lunch hour, a plastic container of cheesecake swirl brownies between us as we sat on the cement stairs behind Pilot Bay High. The snow swirled lazily below us, but we were sheltered near the door. At least it was quiet here.

"Says the girl who has sworn off boys until graduation." I licked my fingers clean of brownie and continued typing on the laptop balanced on my knees.

"Well, yes. I meant *boys*. Skinny, pimply, awkward boys. I'm not sure Gavin even qualifies as a boy."

I gave her a raised eyebrow.

"That, my darling, is a man. And, oh, look at the time, I have to be somewhere." Neve got to her feet and brushed brownie crumbs off her red jeans.

"What are you talking about? Where do you need to be?" I pushed my glasses up on my nose.

"Somewhere *eeelse*," she sang. "Oh, hello, Gavin. Help yourself to a cheesecake brownie."

"What? Traitor," I hissed, cutting off abruptly as Gavin settled himself on the step beside me. There were inches between us, but I could feel the heat from him in the chilly February air.

"So, Audrey." He picked out a brownie from the container.

"Gavin," I answered, pretending to peer at my screen. I'd lost all train of thought but was determined to play it cool. Who knew what reason he had for finding me?

"I wasn't sure you even knew who I was." Gavin took a bite of cheesecake and his eyes widened. "This is amazing. What is it?"

"Neve's latest creation. Of course I know who you are. There are only forty-three students in grade twelve. I know who everyone is."

He considered this as he finished the brownie.

"Can I help you with something?" I meant to say it snarkily, still attempting to play it cool, but it came out a little breathless and he smiled at me. Heaven help me, that smile should come with a warning: May cause dizziness and weak knees, don't look at while operating machinery.

"I think we should go out."

"What?" It came out as more of a squeak than a question. "Like, on a date?"

"No, on a top-secret mission." He laughed. I gave him my best cold stare.

"Yes, on a date, Audrey. Come out for coffee or something with me."

"Why?" I searched his face for any hint that he was messing with me. "We've never even hung out."

"Well, you're gorgeous, of course."

"Hmmm." I blushed. "Continue."

He laughed. "And funny." His green eyes turned serious. "You're smart. You're not afraid of what people think of you. You hardly ever speak up in class, but I'm always waiting to hear what you'll say. I think the history teacher is afraid of you, you know."

"Then he should teach a more balanced, global perspective," I muttered.

"I just want to get to know you better. I promise not to bite. We can go to Pie in the Sky, and Neve can keep you safe." He gave me that deadly smile.

"You know who Neve is?"

"There are only a hundred and eighty-four students in this school," he said. "I know who everyone is."

The bell rang, signaling the end of lunch. I shut my laptop with a snap and stood. Gavin stood too, and when I turned to go, still flustered by the entire encounter, he grabbed my free hand, turning me to face him. I stood a step higher and he was still taller than me.

"Audrey Powell. Come for coffee with me. Just one time." He ran his thumb across the back of my hand, and I shivered. "Or do you not drink coffee?"

I laughed. He obviously didn't know me all that well.

"Oh, I drink coffee."

"Pie in the Sky. Four o'clock." He still held my hand in his, and I felt the contact through my entire body.

I looked down at his hand holding mine, the edges of his tattoo peeking out from the cuff of his dark shirt. I knew I was making him work for it. There could only be one answer, and it had been welling up inside me since he sat down beside me. But I had a feeling this was the moment when everything would change. It was a moment to be savored.

He leaned forward and whispered into my ear, his breath stirring my hair. "Say yes."

This boy. How could anyone say no to this boy? I'd reached the end of my ability to try.

"Yes."

CHAPTER 6

"OH, GOOD, YOU'RE AWAKE."

"Am I?" Blearily, I tried to open my eyes. I vaguely remembered stumbling after Gavin through the snow, getting colder and colder until I didn't even feel the cold anymore. It was all a bit fuzzy.

Speaking of fuzzy...

I sat up and the red cloak slid off the sleeping bag tucked around me. I patted the bedding, looking for my glasses, and realized I was lying on an inflatable camping mattress, the kind that rolls up for backpacking. I found my glasses and the world snapped into focus as I slipped them on. We appeared to be in a cave. Gavin balanced a kettle over a fire near the entrance where I could see early morning light streaming in. How had we gotten here?

"Looking for something?"

I was still feeling around the sleeping bag. "I just…I woke up in the night. I thought I was wrapped up in something furry."

"Hmm." Gavin rummaged around in a backpack and pulled out a travel mug. Didn't seem very faerieish. Actually, everything in the cave looked like camping gear from the local outdoor gear shop.

"Where are we? How did we get here?" I crawled out of the sleeping bag and wrapped the cloak around me.

"This is my cave."

"You don't say."

"And I carried you here after you got all mumbly and stumbly with hypothermia. You're welcome."

"Pretty sure I'm not thanking you for knocking me through a portal to a frozen mountainside and then pulling me off a cliff and stranding me on the frozen mountainside."

Gavin sighed and gave me a look that said it was too early in the morning for arguing with me. Silly boy, it was never too early to be annoyed with him.

I inspected the cave more closely. It was fairly small. Small enough for the little fire to start warming the space up. One side of the cave was heaped with boxes of protein bars and camping supplies, backpacks, and a couple of duffel bags. It looked more like a storehouse than a place to live.

"Coffee?" he asked, interrupting my thoughts.

I gave him my full attention.

"Or I have hot chocolate, tea…I might have some chicken broth somewhere…"

"I'm sorry, I didn't hear anything you said after *coffee*."

"I should have guessed."

"Less talking, more coffeeing."

Gavin snorted in what might have been amusement and pulled a bag of pre-ground coffee beans out of a box. A few minutes later, a cup of steaming, dark-roasted goodness was nestled in my hands.

"Thank you," I breathed, inhaling the steam happily.

"Oh, so now I get a thank you?"

"Shhhhh." I sipped the coffee and closed my eyes. Pre-ground beans were never the best, but it still tasted pretty good. Dark with hints of nuttiness. "I'll consider forgiving you now."

"Because I'm the one who needs to be forgiven?" Gavin squinted at me in annoyance, then stomped out of the cave. Seemed a bit overkill.

For the life of me, I couldn't see what I'd done to him. He was the one who had dragged me out here and given me hypothermia. Not to mention dumping me the week before prom. Still, the coffee was nice.

A minute later, Gavin returned with a small cardboard box. "Breakfast?" He sat down beside me on the mat and handed me a fork. Actually, on closer inspection, it was a spork. Very efficient.

"Is that one of Neve's cheesecakes? I see you believe in covering all the food groups in the morning."

"It has raspberries in it." Gavin took a big bite, and with a shrug, I joined in. Who was I to turn down Neve's baking? The cake was partially frozen. He must have a stash of food buried in a snowbank.

"Why do you have a cheesecake in your secret cave?" I asked through a bite of creamy goodness.

"There's no cheesecake in Faerie." Gavin made short work of his half of breakfast. "I'd never had it until that time at school. I thought I'd died and gone to heaven. I tried to play it cool so you wouldn't think I was strange. Never having eaten cheesecake before."

"Oh, yes, *that's* what would have been strange about you."

He scraped the bottom of the box with his plastic spork to catch any crumbs that might have escaped. "I'm sure you must have questions."

"So many. I don't even know where to start. What were two…werewolf faeries…doing in my high school?"

"*Faoladh*," Gavin said. "Fae who have been cursed to take the form of a wolf from sunset to sunrise. And there are five of us in Pilot Bay, actually. Dylan and I were the ones assigned to your grade."

I seemed to remember other "exchange students" at Pilot Bay High, but I didn't really pay much attention to younger boys. Although, apparently, they weren't high schoolers at all. I took another sip of hot coffee and gave Gavin a sidelong look. Was he even eighteen, like me? "That doesn't answer my question, though."

"It's…complicated."

"I'm a pretty smart girl. I think I can keep up."

"The *faoladh* are the servants of Queen Moriath. Moriath gained the unseelie throne through treachery many years ago. But recently, she's learned that the royal family were not all killed as she'd believed. The youngest daughter may still be alive, in hiding."

"She thinks there's a faerie princess…at Pilot Bay High?" My mind ran through the faces of the girls at my high school. "That's crazy. And I thought you said it happened a long time ago?"

"Like I said, time runs more slowly in your world. We were sent to get to know the students, look for signs that one of them could be her."

Well, I supposed that explained why he'd been interested in me in the first place. Simply on a mission to learn about the kids at the high school. As much as I wanted to believe I was over him, that thought still stung.

"Huh. And that's what you were talking about with Dylan? Your queen is after Isobel Watson?"

"I'm not actually sure what that's about. Kylian just told us the Queen wanted her kept away from the

Rose Gate. If Moriath believed Isobel was the lost princess, she would be dead already."

I shivered.

"So, you're like a minion of the evil queen."

"Pretty much."

"But Dylan is a worse minion of the evil queen."

"Correct."

"Hmmm." I sipped my coffee and considered this. "Why couldn't he see me? In the snow yesterday. This cloak is bright red, and yet he didn't seem to know where I was until I made a noise."

"It's the Cloak of Clíodhna." Gavin picked up the hem and ran his finger across the thick gold embroidery. "I recognize it from the stories my mother used to tell me. It belonged to Aoife the thief. She used it to steal treasures from dragons and trolls, then gave the treasure to those in need. They were some of my favorite bedtime stories. My mom always said the cloak was real, but it's been lost for over five hundred years."

"How does it work?" I fingered the plush velvet with my free hand.

"It causes anyone who sees you to see what they expect to see. Dylan didn't know where you were, or if you were even nearby at all. He mostly expected to see more snow."

"So, not a cool invisibility cloak like in Harry Potter." I took another sip of coffee. "This sounds trickier. How can a cloak be magical?"

"See the thread? It's plated with gold. A powerful magic user can enchant gold, silver, or gems. Gold is most commonly used, although silver makes the best weapons. Gold is too soft."

I examined the knotwork embroidery. Whenever I stared at it for long, it did that twirly thing it'd done at Miss Chloe's house. That must be the magic.

"Magical items can only be made in Faerie, where there's magic all around us. But they can be used in your world, which again makes me curious. Where did you get this cloak in Pilot Bay?"

Clearly, there was more to Miss Chloe than met the eye. But if Gavin worked for an evil faerie queen, it didn't seem wise to bring the librarian to her attention. I examined the cloak in silence. The gold needlework was so intricate. Did the pattern have anything to do with the spell? Was only power needed for enchantments, or was there a skill to it? Was it a combination of ingredients, like making a pie? Or was it precise and logical like coding?

"What do you see when I'm wearing this?" I flipped the hood up and looked over at Gavin. His gold plugs were back in place, making him look deceptively familiar.

"Trouble," he said.

I rolled my eyes. "You should talk."

I finished up the cheesecake, turning over the "evil minion" information in my mind. As badly as Gavin had hurt me, it didn't seem possible that he was actually dangerous. But there was obviously a lot I didn't know about him. All things considered, it seemed wisest to get home as soon as possible. Which, unfortunately, circled back to trusting the boy who broke my heart.

"All right, what's the plan?" I finally asked. "Is it safe yet to trek back to the portal thingy? Do you have any extra winter boots in this secret cave? Snow pants? Or just cheesecake?"

Gavin sighed and leaned back against the cave wall. He was awfully close. My treacherous instincts were having trouble remembering we hated him and wanted to snuggle up against him, maybe lean my head on his shoulder. It was exhausting keeping my distance.

"Dylan following us here complicated things. He may still be waiting on the other side of the gate, or he might have already told Kylian."

"And telling this Kylian is…bad?"

"Kylian is the queen's Huntsman. He commands the *faoladh* and is single-minded in his mission to find the princess. He feels responsible for her escape in the first place and needs to redeem himself to the queen. Not only have I broken at least three of his commands in the past day, but I've also disappeared in the middle of a mission. He is not likely to feel merciful. And he is not likely to be happy about you being the cause of my desertion. Dylan attacking you in the woods would have gotten him a stern lecture on drawing attention to the pack. But Dylan is the pack alpha, and he thinks he's above the rules. Usually he gets away with it. Me running away…well, I'm more likely to become intimately acquainted with his silver axe."

"Bad then." I drank the last of my coffee, tipping the mug up to get every life-giving drop. "Do you have a plan? You seem like someone who"—I waved my hand to take in the cave stuffed with emergency supplies—"plans. Or possibly you're an apocalypse prepper."

Gavin shot me a long look, then gathered up the cheesecake box and our sporks. "I do have a plan." He got to his feet. "But you're not going to like it."

CHAPTER 7

ONE COFFEE DATE WITH GAVIN HAD LED to two, and after two we started spending most of our free time together. Once I got over being flustered, dating Gavin was surprisingly fun. He'd never heard of anime and was truly terrible at computer games, but he was happy to try anything I threw at him.

We watched movies and went for hikes. We hung out with Neve, who smugly gave me "I told you so" looks. My parents muttered about the tattoos and piercings, but he charmed them by calling my dad "Sir", and always having me home before dark.

For a month, he did nothing but hold my hand. Once, he kissed my cheek—and I thought of nothing else the next day but the feel of his lips on my skin. I wondered if he was waiting for me to make the first move, but I wasn't sure how. My previous experience with boys had been limited, and none of it had prepared me for how I felt about Gavin.

One day we were out for a hike after school. There was a trail across the highway from town leading up the mountainside to a lookout. We sat on the low stone wall and felt the early spring sun heat our bones as we stared down at Pilot Bay and the lake stretching out into the distance below.

Gavin swung a leg over the wall and turned to face me. He leaned closer. His cheek brushed against mine and I felt his breath against my ear. Pulling back, he revealed a pale blue wildflower he'd picked from behind me, the first one I'd seen this year. He tucked it behind my ear, and I shivered as his long fingers brushed through my hair.

His gaze dropped to my mouth and he leaned forward. It was a perfectly magical moment.

"You're not going to get in my pants!" I blurted.

Gavin froze. "I..."

"I'm not having sex with you," I clarified, continuing to make this moment as awkward as humanly possible.

"I'm not trying to get in your pants?" Gavin leaned back.

"Right, I know. I'm just... I thought I should let you know." I closed my eyes, wondering if anyone had ever been as good at ruining a romantic interlude as I was. "I'm waiting...until I'm married."

"Okay," said Gavin, steadily.

"Because I—okay?"

"I'm really just trying to kiss you. Have I given you any indication otherwi—"

I cut him short by pressing my lips against his. He recovered quickly and kissed me back. In that moment, I felt myself falling so hard for that sweet boy. His kisses tasted like cheesecake and the promise of happiness with a hint of danger.

When he dropped me off at my house, he kissed me again. He told me he loved me.

And like a fool, I believed him.

"You were right," I yelled at Gavin's back as we hiked down the mountain. "I don't like this plan."

The gist of it was this: other faerie gates existed. Hopefully Kylian wouldn't be watching them. None of them were close by. In fact, the nearest one was at least a two day hike.

So, I traded my small pack for a backpacking one that matched Gavin's. We loaded ourselves up with all sorts of survival gear, and he found me a pair of pants— much too big—along with a pair of boots—also much too big—that I could only keep on my feet with giant thermal socks—which fit perfectly. Just kidding. They were much too big. I wore a thermal shirt with the sleeves rolled up, and the cloak over it all. For style points.

Three hours later, we were nearly down the mountain and out of the snow. I slipped on a patch of muddy slush and landed on my butt. At this rate, I'd need to get the cloak dry-cleaned before I gave it to Neve.

"Is it time to make camp for the night?" I called. Getting up felt like a lot of effort.

Gavin came back up the trail and offered me a hand. "It's barely lunchtime. Let's get down to where it's less mucky and we can take a break."

"Who knew you were so very outdoorsy," I complained, grabbing his wrist.

"I have hidden depths." He winked and hauled me up. For a moment, I pressed flush against him. I would have stepped back immediately but I was…tired. Yes, tired was what I was feeling.

He broke contact first, dropping my hand and turning back to the deer trail he called a path.

I gave my cheek a slap. *Pull it together, Audrey. Only a fool gets her heart broken twice by the same boy.*

A little farther down the trail where the ground was less soggy, we found a couple of comfy-looking rocks and stopped for lunch. I stripped off the borrowed boots and socks and changed back into my trusty red chucks. The cool air in the forest around us felt like early autumn, with the leaves on the giant moss-covered trees just turning yellow and red. Hopefully we were done with the ice and snow.

Gavin handed me a protein bar and a handful of dried fruit.

"How nourishing," I murmured, taking a swig from my water bottle in anticipation of all that dried food.

Gavin just grunted and sat down on a rock nearby.

"So, wolf boy…"

"*Faoladh.*"

"That. Why do you have a cave full of emergency camping supplies? Not that I'm complaining." I bit into my protein bar and grimaced. Unwrinkling the wrapper, I read *Macadamia Cricket Energy Bar.* "Well, actually, I might be complaining a bit. Do you have anything for lunch that's not made of bugs?"

"Nope." Gavin had already finished his bar and started in on his fruit. The boy could eat, that was for sure. "I got a case for a great price on sale."

"I can't imagine why they'd have to discount these." I took another bite and shuddered.

"I've been planning to leave the pack for a while," Gavin said around a mouthful of dried apricot. "It seemed wise to stockpile some supplies while I had the chance. Discipline has been a little laxer since we've been living in Pilot Bay. I've been waiting for the right moment to get away."

I squinted at the trees around us while I listened. I could see little winged shapes darting about. They didn't move like butterflies. Tiny faeries? I blinked and they disappeared. Hmm. I turned back to Gavin.

"Being an evil minion isn't as much fun as advertised?" I asked.

"Not really."

"Is that all you're going to give me?" I choked down the rest of my lunch with a large swig of water.

"I'm just…I'm not used to talking about it. I've never actually had anyone I could share this with. Still hungry?" Gavin offered me another foil-wrapped bar, but I waved it away.

"Then you're in luck," I told him. "I'm an excellent listener."

"I thought you wanted to push me off a cliff."

I may have said something to that effect a couple of hours back.

"I'm much too tired and malnourished for that sort of thing now. Come on. Tell me why you don't want to work for the evil queen anymore. How did you end up as a minion in the first place? Did you grow up as a roly poly wolf cub in her evil lair?"

"I grew up in a small castle in the mountains, actually, but my family spent most of our time at Skyretaine in the court of the Unseelie King. My parents, my older brother, Ruarc, and me. When Moriath took the throne, my parents, along with a number of the *Tuatha Dé Danann,* hastily pledged fealty and then slipped away from court. I was still a child at the time."

"I'm already lost." I leaned back against my backpack, tucking the cloak around me for warmth.

"Okay." Gavin settled back against his pack as well. "The *Tuatha Dé Danann* are the high fae. The Faeries that look most similar to humans."

"But with the fun pointy ears."

"Correct. They rule the other fae, the *Aos Sí*."

"Why?"

Gavin sighed. "Because that's how it's always been."

"That's a terrible reason," I pointed out.

"It is." He gave me a look. "Are we going to discuss politics, or can I continue?"

"First, explain what an unseelie is."

"Okay." Gavin sat up and grabbed a stick. "So, this is *Tír na nÓg*." He drew an island in the dirt. "It's the part of Faerie where we are."

I leaned in to watch as he sketched some triangles across the middle of the island.

"These are the *Bhanmhor Sliabhraon*, the mountain range we're climbing down. Most of the land below is the territory of the seelie fae, also known as the summer folk. Their kingdom is split into a number of smaller courts. They sure love their politics, but in the end, they all follow the Seelie King." He poked a spot near the bottom of the island that I assumed was the home of the Seelie King. "The upper lands belong to the unseelie fae, or the winter folk. We tend to be more independent."

"No fancy courts for you?"

"Not minor courts. Just the main one at Skyretaine." He pointed his stick at a spot above the mountain range. "But, like I said, that's not much of a court anymore. Then at the very top of *Tír na nÓg* is the realm of the dwarves." He drew a few more triangles at the top of the island. "Got it?"

"Sure." Dwarves? What about dragons? Unicorns? *Focus, Audrey.* "Where did you grow up?"

Gavin scratched an X into the mountains north of the Unseelie Queen's castle. "About here. So, a few years after we moved back there, our new queen came for a social visit. Or so she said, but of course she was checking to make sure that our loyalty remained hers. My parents warned my brother and me not to trust her. Not in those words—that would be treason—but they warned us to be on our guards. That she might seem lovely, but her attention span was short. And young men who chose to go away with her never returned to their families. No one knew what happened to them."

"You didn't listen?"

"Oh, I did, but you have to understand. Queen Moriath was like no one I'd ever seen. I'd grown up believing her to be fearsome, but she was beautiful. When she asked questions, you could tell she truly cared about your answers. After only a day, we were both more than a little in love with her."

I forced myself to unclench my hands. I'd unconsciously dug my fingernails in hard enough into my palms to leave red half moons behind.

"When we woke the next morning, Moriath was gone." He jabbed his stick into the ground so hard it stuck there. "And so was Ruarc.

"My parents were devastated, and I was numb with shock. I would never have believed Ruarc would leave like that. We'd always been close, especially since leaving Skyretaine, but he left in the night without a word. I believed my parents then. Moriath must have bewitched him and stolen him away."

"What did you do?"

"I followed them, of course. I snuck out the next night while my parents slept. I can't imagine how they must have felt when they realized I was gone, but I was sure I could talk some sense into him, bring him back home.

"I took my horse and a pack of supplies and made my way to the Unseelie Court. I thought I might be able to overtake them on the road, but never did. I arrived at the queen's castle ten days later."

"Was your brother there?"

Gavin laughed humorlessly. "It took me weeks to track him down. Her attention span was even shorter than I could have guessed. Or maybe my brother wasn't all that much fun. She'd tired of him already. I found Ruarc with the rest of the *faoladh*. That's what happened to the young men the queen lured away. They joined her personal wolf pack. I begged him to come home, but he refused. I thought he still loved Moriath. I didn't realize then how difficult it is to walk away from the *faoladh*."

CHAPTER 8

I LEANED FORWARD, COMPLETELY ABSORBED by his story. "Did you go home after you found your brother?"

"That would have been wise." Gavin ran a hand through his hair. "But how could I leave Ruarc there alone? How could I go back to my grief-stricken parents without him?"

"So, you thought you'd leave them without you as well?"

"Great logic, right?" He sighed. "If you'd been there, I'm sure you could have smacked some sense into me. But you weren't. And so, I did the only thing that came to mind. I approached the queen and asked to join him."

"What did she say?" I tried to pull my mind away from the mental picture of Gavin with some icy fae lady.

"She laughed at first. I was still very young, barely out of childhood. Doubtless why she hadn't bothered with me in the first place."

"You and she didn't…" I couldn't bring myself to ask outright.

"No! No. She accepted my vow of fealty and I joined the *faoladh* that night."

My chest unclenched a little. "What did your brother think?"

"He raged at me. Told me I was an idiot. But he wasn't angry for long." Gavin scuffed the dirt with his booted foot.

"He forgave you?" Where was his brother now? Was he in Pilot Bay too?

"He was killed in a border skirmish six months later. The seelie crown prince himself cut him down in battle." Gavin spat on the ground.

"Oh." I winced. "And you've been stuck with the evil wolf minions for…a while?"

"A long while," he confirmed. "I'd about given up on trying to find a way out, until someone reminded me there was more to life than pain and death. That maybe I could hope for something better."

I perked up. "Someone?"

"A mouthy, blonde someone with violent tendencies." He stood and peered down the mountainside.

"Hmmm…" I tapped my chin. "I don't know anyone by that description. But if someone reminds you to hope, it doesn't seem like you should dump them the day before prom…"

Gavin ignored me and swung his pack back on. "Come on. We have a lot of ground to cover before nightfall."

Apparently, I hiked more slowly than Gavin had anticipated. One minute I was following Gavin down the path, the sun disappearing behind the mountain, and in the next, a large black wolf had taken his place.

I didn't scream. I wasn't the screaming type. But it was possible I yelped in a casual, non-screaming fashion. It's not that I hadn't believed him about the wolf thing, but it was something else to see the transformation with my own eyes.

He stopped and turned, giving me what was certainly an ironic wolf look, waiting to see my reaction. I managed to regain my composure. Mostly.

"You're a wolf."

He opened his mouth in a wolfy smile. There were a lot of teeth in there.

"You don't talk when you're a wolf?"

He just turned and continued down the trail, padding along.

"Hmm…could be worse, I suppose." I jogged a pace to catch up. "I see why you had me carry the tent.

Um, your backpack will reappear in the morning, yes? And your clothes?"

The wolf came to a sudden stop, growling lightly, and I nearly toppled over him.

Ahead lay the valley where he'd planned to camp for the night, but the valley wasn't empty. A campfire burned merrily away, and I could hear laughter.

It sounded awfully nice, but the most enticing thing by far was the scent of roasting meat wafting over on the breeze. It smelled like roast chicken, only better. My mouth watered, and my stomach growled. They both remembered the unsatisfying lunch they'd eaten. Supper was going to be more of the same.

Why should I eat protein bars made of bugs when other people—friendly people, by the sounds of things—had roast chicken?

My brain was still considering, but my body had made up its mind. I passed Gavin and picked up my pace down the mountainside. Only to be jerked to a stop by my cloak. I glanced back. Gavin had his teeth closed over the hem of my cloak. He growled quietly and shook his head.

"Okay," I told him, "I know it's not smart to take food from strangers. But what if they sound like really nice strangers, and the only food you have is made out of crickets? I would say these are extenuating circumstances."

Gavin just growled again.

"If you can explain to me why I shouldn't go down there, I'll stop right now."

He glared at me, still holding onto my cloak with his teeth.

"What's that you say? Nothing?"

He took a step back, dragging me with him.

I sighed. "Fine, fine, but the next time we go on an adventure, I'm in charge of the food."

He let go and left the trail, and I reluctantly followed him into the woods.

Suddenly, I was stopped short again as two figures stepped out of the tree's shadows. Each grabbed one of my arms in an iron grip. This time I may have screamed more then yelped. I looked for Gavin, but he'd disappeared into the dark forest.

"Won't you join us by the fire?" said a low, female voice in my ear. I felt the press of a knife to my throat and gulped.

Maybe not so friendly after all.

CHAPTER 9

AKE HER BACK TO THE CAMP. I'LL find the wolf," said my other captor, also female. She released my arm and faded into the shadows.

"Come along then," murmured the woman in an Irish-sounding accent. Another faerie?

She marched me at knife point through the trees until we reached the campfire. Someone was telling a story, which was apparently hilarious due to the laughter and hooting from his audience. All the noise came to a sudden stop when I was thrust forward into the circle of fae sitting around the crackling fire.

Four pairs of eyes fixed on me. The storyteller, a burly fae man with a full black beard, stopped with his arms still in mid gesture, mouth gaping.

I must have looked a sight with my over-sized shirt, red chucks, rolled-up hiking pants, and velvet cloak. My hood was up, covering my very human ears, but that wasn't enough to make me blend in with this group in all their leather and fur.

"Orla," said a pale, redheaded fae man. "Do introduce us to this lovely maiden you seem to have found out in the forest. Is she friendly?"

"I brought her to you to find out," Orla replied, easing her knife away from my neck. She correctly guessed I wouldn't be foolish enough to bolt when I was so obviously outnumbered.

"How fascinating." The redheaded man leaned back against the log, looking comfortably in charge.

I, on the other hand, was freaking out. Why had I—even briefly—thought it would be a good idea to approach a bunch of strange fae? Gavin had seemed afraid of them, and he was a wolf. What would they do to a human girl?

"I don't recognize you, lass. What court do you belong to?"

I looked around the circle of fae. None of them seemed shocked by my strange appearance. Why? Oh, I'd forgotten the magic of the cloak. I fingered the embroidered edge. What did they see when they looked at me? Probably what they expected to, according to Gavin. If the man was asking about my court, they must assume I was one of them. The *Tuatha Dé Danann*, Gavin had called them.

"Um…" They were still waiting for me to answer. Which court? If Gavin didn't like them, and he was unseelie, then these fae were probably… "Seelie?"

A fierce-looking woman with dark brown skin scanned me with narrowed eyes. "Tiernan, you can't trust this girl. A lone seelie fae this far over the mountains? Who doesn't recognize you, the crown prince?"

I froze. The seelie crown prince? The fae who had killed Gavin's brother? Heart pounding, I looked around the circle of fae again, this time noting how they bristled with daggers. Bows and swords lay within easy reach. The bearded man fiddled with a gleaming silver axe.

I swallowed and forced myself to breathe. Running was not an option here. I'd have to fake my way through this.

"Um, of course I recognize you from your-…paintings?" I didn't know much about *Tír na nÓg,* but it seemed unlikely they had the internet here. "I was just surprised. Your Highness." I attempted a curtsy. It was probably terrible, as I'd never curtsied before. Was I supposed to curtsy? "I was traveling home, when a wolf chased me into the forest." That was the truth at least.

The redheaded prince gave Orla a sharp look over my head. "Wolf?"

"One of the unseelie *faoladh.* Rian is hunting for it now," said Orla.

Prince Tiernan let out a low whistle. "Well, lass, it seems lucky for you that Orla found you." He gave me a charming smile. I tried to stay calm. "What did you say your name was?"

"Audrey…your Highness?" Of course I sounded unsure about the only part of my story that was actually true. I'd make a terrible spy.

"Oh, we don't need to be formal." The prince waved a freckled hand. "Not out here in the wilds."

"Tiernan," warned the fierce woman. "I—"

"She's one maiden, Sersh, and we're an entire *fianna*. I think we can risk it." Tiernan motioned to the spot beside him by the fire. "Come, sit. Calder, give the lass some food. Orla, quit hovering. She's a tiny thing. She's not about to overpower me."

I mean, I was five-foot eight, but I supposed that was short compared to the fae lounging around the fire. I nervously sat on the ground beside the prince, spreading the cloak under me. I kept my hood up and my rounded ears covered, not sure how much to trust the magic of the cloak.

"We should have introductions," exclaimed Tiernan, rubbing his hands together. "It's so rare to have guests out on patrol."

Orla rolled her eyes. Now that she was across the fire from me, I could get a better look at her. She was dressed, as they all were, in leather pants, with high boots and a long brown coat. She watched me through narrowed eyes as someone handed her a skewer of food.

How much of my casual conversation with Gavin had she heard? Clearly, she was having trouble believing my story, but she didn't seem to feel it was worth arguing over with Tiernan. It was probably as Tiernan had said—I didn't look like much of a threat. That was most likely the reason I was still alive.

"You've already met Orla, of course, and her sister Rian," Tiernan began. Nothing about the way he was dressed indicated any status, but he was obviously used to having his way. "They're twins, if you can believe it."

"I...can?"

"And here's Calder with your food. Thank you, Calder."

A thin, pale man handed me a skewer of roast meat and vegetables with a wide grin. I gulped and pulled back sharply. The fae smiled with rows of thin, needle-sharp fangs.

"Don't mind the teeth." Teirnan took the skewer with a smile at the man. "Calder's grandmother on his father's side was a *Dearg Du*. But he hardly ever drinks blood."

"It's much too salty," mumbled Calder as he retreated to the other side of the fire.

"Calder is an excellent cook." Tiernan handed me the skewer. "He packs all sorts of herbs and salt and things along on patrol. We used to take turns preparing meals, but Calder has forbidden the rest of us from cooking. Well…mostly me."

My stomach rumbled at the smell of roasted meat and root vegetables. I cautiously nibbled the meat. It did taste like chicken a bit, but darker and more complex with fragrant herbs coating it.

"It's really good, Calder, thank you." I felt a bit bad for jumping. I hadn't meant to be rude. It was just a lot of teeth.

"The trick is to rub it all with salt and fat before cooking," the cook explained.

"Next is Saoirse." Tiernan pronounced it *Searshah*. "She's like a sister to me."

"Like a sister who was traded to the Seelie Court as a hostage against her people's good behavior and never allowed to return to her homeland?" asked the brown-skinned woman, raising an eyebrow at Tiernan.

"Yes, like that sort of sister. Only that sounds terrible, and you know I don't think of you that way." Tiernan turned back to me. "My father...well, I'm sure you know enough about the Seelie King. Let's not ruin our dinner. Moving on. Fergus!"

The bearded man across the fire from me started.

"Not only is Fergus deadly with an axe, he can name any bird in the forest, just by hearing it. Isn't that right, Fergus?"

"Well..." Fergus began.

"What's that creepy screeching sound? Owl?"

Fergus sighed. "A barn owl."

"And that buzzing one?"

"Nightjar."

"What about the chittery sound?"

"That's a squirrel, Tiernan."

"He could be making it all up for all we can tell," said Tiernan in a mock whisper to me.

I stifled a giggle. He made it hard to stay nervous.

"I would never lie about birds," muttered Fergus, jotting something down in a little notebook. "It corrupts the data."

"Unfortunately, the rest of the *fianna* is off on other duties," said Tiernan.

"Oh, are we calling Declan being dragged off by his mother to compete for the hand of a princess a duty now?" Saoirse laughed.

"To be fair, Declan's mother is terrifying." Tiernan grimaced and Saoirse nodded in begrudging agreement.

I'd finished my skewer by that point and was examining the sharpened stick the food had been cooked on. Tiernan plucked it from my fingers and handed it back to Calder. For all his friendly banter, his trust did have limits it seemed.

If he decided to ask more questions of me, I knew I couldn't answer them to the satisfaction of anyone around the fire. I was depending on the sketchy magic of the cloak and my vague answers to keep my secrets.

Despite Gavin's story, I almost wondered if I should just tell them the truth. Maybe they could help me get home? But the number of weapons around the fire kept me silent. It was too much of a risk.

Thinking of Gavin, I scanned the forest, hoping Rian hadn't found him out there. But I couldn't see anything past the campfire. I was night blind from the light.

After dodging a couple more questions from Tiernan, I managed a large yawn and a couple of slow blinks.

"Ah, lass, you must be exhausted from your excitement today," said Tiernan kindly. "Why don't you sleep here with us tonight, and we'll sort out what to do with you in the morning."

I nodded sleepily, and they found me a place in the moss not far from the fire. I used my pack as a pillow and spread my cloak over me. Luckily, the fire kept the chill away, because pulling out my very sporty tent and sleeping bag seemed like it would be pushing the limits of what the cloak could handle.

I pretended to sleep, and might have actually dozed a bit, as I waited for the group to settle in for the night. I heard Fergus continue the story I'd interrupted earlier—something about a lazy man with an enchanted purse—and there was singing. Saoirse had a beautiful, lilting voice.

At one point I woke from a doze to hear Rian return. She told Tiernan she'd lost the wolf, and I felt something inside me unclench.

Finally, the fire burned down to glowing embers and the warriors made their beds around it. I waited until all the tossing and murmuring settled down. And then I waited some more. At last, satisfied that everyone around the fire was asleep, I rose silently with my pack and crept away from the campfire.

Should I just ask Tiernan and his friends for help? Surely they could find a faerie gate and help me get home. While I hesitated, a pair of eyes appeared just beyond the edge of the clearing, reflecting the light of the glowing fire. Gavin.

I started walking toward the wolf. But why? Why did I still trust him? How did I know he wouldn't break my heart again when he showed no remorse for doing it the first time? My brain had all sorts of things to say, but my feet kept walking.

"I know what you are, human girl," a voice hissed behind me

I jumped at least a foot into the air and spun to find Calder standing there. Of course they'd set a guard. They were a band of elite warriors, not Cub Scouts.

"I don't know what you mean," I said inanely.

"You might be able to trick our eyes, girl, but I can smell your blood. And I can smell that you've been travel-ing with the *faoladh* for some time now." He smiled and revealed all those pointed teeth, which glinted in the moonlight. He raised his hand and the moonlight outlined a sharp point. I stumbled back, wondering if Gavin would make it in time to save me.

"For your wolf friend," he said a bit ominously, then handed me the sharpened stick. It was covered with roasted meat. Leftovers from dinner. Calder was helping me.

"But, why?" I asked, accepting the food from him.

Calder shrugged. "I have a good feeling about you. And if you trust the wolf, that's your business. He's far from his queen and his pack out here."

"Thank you," I said simply.

"Go now, before someone hears you. Someone with more questions. And I'd avoid strange campfires as you travel deeper into unseelie territories. I don't know what your friend has told you, but most faeries you meet in these lands won't be content to feed you dinner and tell you stories."

I shivered and nodded. I hesitated, but he turned and walked back to the fire. Whirling around, I half ran the last few steps to the dark forest where my wolf waited for me.

CHAPTER 10

WHEN I REACHED GAVIN, HE BRUSHED up against my legs with a low growl I took to mean he was happy to see me, but still annoyed I'd foolishly gotten captured in the first place. I offered him the skewer of meat, which he ignored. Either he didn't trust the seelie fae, or he was a big fan of cricket protein.

Enough moonlight filtered through the trees that after a bit my eyes adjusted, and I could follow Gavin's dark shape. Making camp was apparently off the table with the enemy nearby, so we trekked through the night.

After a couple hours of hiking, I started to stumble in my tiredness. I considered myself to be in half decent shape—I mean, I walked everywhere—but this had been a *lot* of walking.

The forest began to lighten with the first hints of morning when I tripped over a tree root and landed on my hands and knees in soggy earth. Lovely. A boggy marshland stretched out ahead. Gavin's furry form paced just ahead of me. He must be trying to decide what the best way across or around would be.

I rose into a crouch to wipe my hands on the moss and then almost fell backward when a flash of light appeared in front of my nose. My hood slid down, and I widened my eyes in surprise. The flash of light widened its tiny eyes right back at me. It was a little person, about as tall as my pinky finger, and quite round. It glowed so brightly that I couldn't make out what it wore, or much else about it but floating hair and wispy wings. A misty glow surrounded it, swirling in lazy eddies as it moved.

The little figure floated a few inches away from me, waving at me to follow. As I got to my feet, dozens more little misty faeries popped up across the predawn swamp, like twinkle lights along a garden path.

I straightened and stepped forward without really thinking about what I was doing. The little light flickered happily and floated back another foot, waiting for me to follow. I took another step, but before I could go farther, a firm hand pulled me back against a warm chest.

"You need to stop being so trusting," Gavin whispered in my ear.

The first rays of sunlight lit the forest around us, revealing a swamp that was far less solid than I'd thought. The path of dancing lights led straight to a dark pool of water in its center.

"Shoo, *Sheerie*." Gavin swatted at the little faerie.

The wispy light in front of me gave an annoyed squeak and darted out to meet its fellow faeries above the swamp. More little lights joined them, and they flitted and danced, skating along the surface of the water and twirling between reeds and snags of tree branches. Even after realizing that they'd been trying to drown me in the swamp, it was impossible to take my eyes off the beautiful display.

But I'd always had a terrible sense of self-preservation, which was clear by the fact that I didn't step away from Gavin's warmth. He kept his arms around me and said next to my ear, "Those are the *Sheerie*. Sometimes they'll help a lost traveler, but more often they'll lead you to your doom. It's not wise to trust them, unless you have something to bargain with."

I shivered. And yet... "They're beautiful."

The little faeries disappeared one by one in the light of dawn. Where did they go?

"You should know by now that looks can be deceiving," Gavin said softly, his breath stirring the hair by my ear. He skimmed his hand down my arm, and I felt it more than should have been possible through the velvet of my cloak.

"I really should." I stepped away from him pointedly, but his hand caught mine. With a twist he spun me around to face him.

He twirled the pink tips of my hair with his free hand, holding me fast with the other. But what truly kept me from pulling away again was the unguarded look in his dark eyes.

"You have to understand, Audrey, I never wanted to hurt you. I was only trying to keep you safe." His thumb brushed across my knuckles. "And a great job I did at that. I should have left you alone from the start."

"Why didn't you?" What on earth had possessed a fae boy to ask me out?

He leaned down and whispered with a brush of his lips against mine. "I tried."

I shuddered but pulled back far enough to see his face. "You tried? You're the one who started all this. You're the one who asked me out for coffee in the first place. Why?" All the pain came welling up again, until I struggled to take a breath. "Why would you tell me you loved me if you were just going to leave me? How was that keeping me safe?"

Gavin sighed and leaned his forehead against mine.

"I know. It was selfish of me. It's just… I'd been with the *faoladh*, working for the Unseelie Queen, for so long. I saw horrible things and was powerless to stop them. I…" He hesitated. "People died, some of them at my hand. The only way to survive was to pretend to be like the rest of them. To act like I didn't care about anything. And the longer I pretended, the harder it was to tell who I really was anymore. But then we got sent to Pilot Bay, and there you were." He looked down at me again. "The first time I saw you, you made me smile. The first time we spoke, you made me laugh. I'd been trapped in the dark for so long, and you were like this shining light. I couldn't stay away from you."

His words cut into me. I wanted to let all the pain go and pull him down for a kiss. But I still hurt, so badly. I couldn't pull down those walls around my heart. I couldn't get hurt like that again.

I stepped back, trying to find enough room to breathe. "And yet, you've done a pretty good job at staying away for the past month."

He still held my hand. "I was drawing too much attention to you. The other *faoladh*, Audrey, they're dangerous. I've seen the games they play with humans who catch their eye. That hiker who went missing last winter—"

"You broke my heart, Gavin," I interrupted him. "You dumped me the day before prom." Maybe after everything, I shouldn't care about prom. But I'd built it up all year in my mind. The dress. The flowers. The boy who'd dance with me all night.

"I was never going to take you to prom, Audrey. It's after dark."

"Yeah, your home by nightfall curfew makes a lot more sense now. But...you just...there was no warning. No explanation. And if your goal was to keep me safe, how did you think leaving me to Dylan would turn out?"

Gavin stiffened and dropped my hand. "Ah yes, Dylan. At least your heartbreak didn't last long, did it?"

I gaped at him. "You're going to turn this back on me? Really?"

"We should probably make camp for a few hours. You must be tired." He turned and scanned the forest, maturely avoiding eye contact. Just like that, he could turn it off again. "Then we'd better head west and avoid the swamp."

I sighed. Heart-to-heart time was apparently over. "How far are we from the gate?"

"Only another couple of hours at our current pace." He pointed through the trees. At more trees. "That way."

"Then why are we stopping?" I pulled the cloak tighter around me, trying to shove down my emotions like he was apparently so good at. "Let's keep going and get home."

"It's not that simple." He took off without further explanation, clearly expecting me to follow along as he hunted for a good campsite.

"Is anything ever simple with you?" I shot back as I jogged to catch up.

"Let's get some sleep, and then I'll explain. This isn't something we should attempt without clear heads."

We found a level, mossy spot to pitch the tent and ate our meal in silence. I munched on the leftover kebab to his silent disapproval.

We crawled into sleeping bags on opposite sides of the tent. Gavin immediately rolled over to sleep. After glaring at his back for a minute, I did the same, falling asleep quickly despite the morning sunlight filtering through the trees and my churning emotions.

Have you ever had your still-beating heart ripped out of your chest, and squeezed to a pulp in front of your eyes?

I have.

Or, at least, that's what it felt like when Gavin had said he thought we shouldn't see each other anymore.

"It's nothing to do with you." He wouldn't meet my eyes. We sat at our regular table at Pie in the Sky, Neve watching from the counter across the cafe.

"What do you mean it's nothing to do with me? That's the stupidest thing I've ever heard!" I got a little unkind when my heart was breaking. "How could it not be about me? I'm the one you don't want to be around anymore."

I hadn't seen it coming. Not at all. Just yesterday, we'd spent the whole day together, watching Star Wars. I thought it strange when he said they didn't have Star Wars in Ireland, but in retrospect, it made more sense. Things had seemed completely normal. Sure, he had been avoiding the topic of prom, but I assumed it was because he thought tuxes were lame.

Not that he thought *I* was lame.

"It's not that I don't want to be around you anymore." He met my eyes then, and it was hard to ignore the obvious pain in them. But I managed, because surely he must be acting. He must have been so good at acting to tell someone he loved them one day and then end it the next with no warning.

I took a sip of coffee. It tasted like...nothing. This stupid boy had me so upset that I couldn't even enjoy coffee.

"How dare you," I muttered, glaring at my mug. The white ceramic cup blurred as I blinked back tears.

He leaned forward. "What?"

"How. Dare. You." I leaned forward as well. "How dare you string me along like that. How dare you pretend to love me!" I dimly noticed that I wasn't using my inside voice anymore. "How dare you break up with me the week before prom with the most cliché line of all time."

Gavin leaned back. The nervous look in his eyes was gratifying.

"It's not me? That's all you've got?"

"Audrey, I—"

Neve appeared at my side. "I think you should go."

He gave her a pleading look.

"Are you going to make this any better by staying?" she asked, hands on her hips.

Gavin opened his mouth, looked at me, and closed it again.

"That's what I thought." She waved her tea towel toward the exit. "Off you go."

I waited until the bell over the door chimed as he left before I started crying. Neve pulled up a chair and wrapped her arms around me as I succumbed to big, ugly sobs.

Neve dragged me to prom the next day and made me dance with her even though stupid boys made catcalls at us from across the gym. I saw the photos later. Neve was a bombshell in her vintage red dress with white polka dots, and I looked beautiful in my Sailor Venus inspired dress, but I didn't feel beautiful. I didn't feel anything at all.

The next Monday at lunch, Dylan asked me if I wanted to go out with him. Of course I didn't want to. I wanted to go home and have another good, pathetic cry.

But there behind him, as always, was Gavin. I tried to ignore him, but that compulsion, that gravity always humming between us, was still there. I watched him, waiting for him to say something. He opened his mouth and said...

Nothing.

He just raised an eyebrow at me, then turned to walk away.

Like he didn't care what I did. Like it didn't matter to him one way or the other.

So, I did the only thing I could think of, the only thing that would make him hurt as badly as he'd hurt me. If he felt anything at all.

I walked up to Dylan, that smug, blond boy, wrapped my arms around his neck, and pulled him down for a kiss.

I'd always thought I was a pretty smart girl, but man, did heartbreak ever make me stupid.

Chapter 11

I WOKE UP TO THE BRIGHT MIDDAY SUN shining through the blue tent fly. The sleeping bag across from me was empty. I lay there for a few minutes, staring at the mesh tent top and contemplating the certainty of cricket protein for breakfast. But then I smelled coffee.

I crawled out of the tent, with a yawn, still in my black Naruto t-shirt and Gavin's rolled up hiking pants. Hopefully I didn't smell funny. Did Gavin have super wolf smelling powers? It would serve him right if I stunk.

Wolf boy hunched over a tiny stove, really just a little fuel tank with a burner on top. I gave him my best morning glare (the actual time of day was immaterial). He quirked an eyebrow at me and handed me a travel mug.

It was awfully hard to be mad at someone who gave you coffee. That's why my fights with Neve never lasted more than a day.

I mumbled a thank you and sat on a mossy, fallen log.

"Hello, gorgeous," I said softly.

"Good morning to you, too." Gavin poured hot water through a mesh coffee filter into a second travel cup.

"Shhh, I was talking to my coffee."

He just laughed. Yesterday's snit was apparently over. I still had no clue why he was so touchy about our breakup. It hadn't been my idea, after all.

After shaking out the coffee grounds and turning off the stove, Gavin settled down on the log beside me with his cup of coffee. He handed me a cricket protein bar. It claimed to be carrot cake.

"I've never eaten bug carrot cake before." I tore it open in resignation.

"I had it yesterday," said Gavin.

"And?"

"I decided it would be cruel of me to not share the remaining one with you."

I took a bite and couldn't help a grimace.

"Maybe if it came with cream cheese icing?" I managed after choking down the mouthful.

"Well, with any luck, I'll get you back to Neve's baking before dark."

"What about you? Don't you need some fresh cheesecake?"

"And give up on cinnamon bun flavored crickets?"

I was relatively sure he was kidding, but the boy had eaten two protein bars by the time I'd worked up the courage to try mine at all.

"So, where's this gate, then?" I took another bite and fought the resulting gag reflex by washing it down with coffee. Poor coffee. It didn't deserve to be mixed with powdered insects.

"The Lichen Gate. It's not far." He looked at the forest speculatively. "Maybe two hours?"

"And then we hop through the gate and go back to Pilot Bay?"

Gavin took a stalling sip of coffee. "Weeeeeeell..."

"Of course. Please, tell me what the catch is."

"The gate is guarded."

I sighed. "Naturally. By what, dragons?"

"Of course not. We're too far south."

"Obviously." I rolled my eyes. "Genie?"

"Does this look like Genie territory?"

"Right, too mossy." I tapped my finger on my chin as Gavin took another sip of coffee. "Evil witch in a gingerbread cottage?"

Coffee sprayed as Gavin choked on a mouthful.

"I was kidding!" I stared at him, appalled. "Wolf boy, please tell me we're not actually hiking toward a gingerbread cottage. I'm not that sick of cricket bars." I considered the empty carrot cake wrapper. "Actually..."

"The Lichen Gate is guarded by an old and powerful fae named Bronach. You could call her a witch, yes. She uses the gate to steal away children from your world. Bronach bewitches kids and sells them to be raised in Faerie as...whatever their buyer wants. Don't try and nibble on her house though. It's not candy."

I stared at him, too horrified to come up with a witty retort.

"But that's terrible!"

"I'm so glad you think so. Because we're going to make it a lot harder for her."

Later that afternoon, we peered out from behind trees dripping with strands of lichen at a charming little cabin in a clearing. When I was a kid, we called lichen witch's hair. That had seemed hilarious, back when I thought witches only existed in Halloween movies. A low stone wall surrounded the cabin, and a tall stone gateway arched over the path leading to the front door. More lichen covered the arch.

"I'm guessing that's the Lichen Gate?" I whispered.

"Good eye," murmured Gavin beside me. "Are you ready?"

"Nope."

Because here was the thing: it wasn't enough that the gate practically sat in the witch's yard. It was also locked. Yes, apparently magic faerie gates could be—and usually were—locked to keep people from stumbling about between realms. Or to keep stolen children from running home.

We needed that key. Not only was it our only hope of escaping through the Lichen Gate, but it would also make it harder for Bronach to move freely through the human world. She could open her own gate without it, but the key allowed her to use all the unseelie gates in the human realm and *Tír na nÓg* at will.

"What if she's not home?" Because of course she needed to be home, or else she'd have the key with her.

"She's home." Gavin pointed at the smoke rising from the chimney. "See that window? The one open a crack? Wait for her to open the door, and then climb through. I'll keep her distracted as long as I can."

I gulped, not at all excited about this plan. But I also didn't want to spend the rest of my life tromping through the forests of Faerie eating cricket protein.

"And then we'll meet back here and wait for nightfall." Gavin glanced back at me. "Got it?"

"Got it."

This would all be simpler if the gate weren't right in front of her house.

"Keep your hood up. The cloak should hide you if you need it." He pulled the velvet hood up over my head, then leaned forward and kissed me. Just a quick brush of his lips on mine.

I froze, stunned. Gavin didn't seem to notice.

"You'll be fine." And with that, he cracked his neck and strode toward the witch's front door.

I knelt to make sure the laces on my chucks were firmly tied, waiting until my heart stopped racing before I stood again. I told myself it was nerves, but honestly, I had no idea how to handle Gavin being sweet again. What had he meant by that kiss? Was it just old habits coming back? Did he still have feelings for me?

I could feel my defenses crumbling, but how could I trust him with my heart again? I'd barely put it back together after the first time.

I shook my head. I had to focus. Romance was a problem for future Audrey to deal with. I took a deep breath and crept across the clearing towards the open window.

The sharp knocking on the door made me jump, even though I'd been waiting for it. Footsteps echoed from inside the house, followed by the creak of the door opening.

"What are you doing here, wolf?" said a low, female voice.

"Lady Bronach, I have a message for you from the Queen."

I eased the window up.

"What does my sister want this time?" she bit out.

Climbing through a window while trying to keep covered by a heavy cloak was awkward to say the least, but I managed not to tumble over the windowsill as I slid to the floor.

"There's a problem with the most recent shipment..." Gavin's voice drifted through the cottage.

I stood in a tidy kitchen, with herbs hanging from the ceiling and a wood stove topped with a bubbling pot in one corner. A smooth wooden table sat in the middle of the room, and shelves lined the walls. If I were a witch, where would I hide a magic key? Gavin had said it would probably not be an actual key, but something gold and small. Easy to carry. Most likely jewelry.

Scanning the shelves, I listened to the conversation at the door with half an ear to be sure the witch was still occupied. I found wooden boxes of lizard tails, a jar of teeth, and several rounds of waxed cheese, but nothing that looked like the key.

I padded through the doorway leading away from the sound of conversation, toward the back of the cottage, and found myself in a room lined with cages. They were built of black, twisted iron, and each had a gold lock on their doors. Varying in size, nearly all sat empty, apart from a couple of sad-looking birds and a sleeping badger. One empty cage held a pink sock, and another a dirty stuffed llama. I shivered. This must be where the witch kept the children she stole from the human world. Where was the owner of that little llama now?

Gavin had said that the best way to stop the witch was to steal her key, but I couldn't help thinking that Hansel and Gretel had the right idea when they shoved their witch into a fireplace.

The iron bars of the nearest cage seemed to twist slightly. Dark patterns formed in the air around them. Something about the shapes reminded me of sleep...and forgetfulness. How could I tell that?

I reached out to see if the cage hummed the way my cloak always did.

"I wouldn't do that if I were you," hissed a female voice.

I practically jumped out of my skin and threw a startled glance over my shoulder at the doorway to the kitchen. Empty.

"Up here, child."

I followed the voice to a cage hanging in a corner of the room. A pair of golden eyes blinked at me from deep in the shadows.

"You're a cat," I said, stupidly.

"I'm a *Cait Sith*," corrected the sleek, black cat with a sniff. "And I'd appreciate it if you'd unlock my cage before you get yourself caught by Bronach."

"I'm looking for her key," I whispered. "The one for the faerie gates."

"Interesting." The cat gave a long, feline blink. "I'll tell you where it is. But first, set me free. The key to the cages is over in that desk. Second drawer."

"Is this a trick?" I didn't see what a cat could do to me, but then, the little *Sheerie* had looked sweet too. "I suppose you wouldn't tell me if it were."

"I suppose I wouldn't," agreed the cat. "But you don't look like the sort of girl who would leave me trapped here."

I sighed. She was right. And my search was getting me nowhere. How long could Gavin keep the witch distracted? I rifled through the desk's second drawer and found a long key forged of black iron. It hummed softly in my hand, casting off those dark patterns again, but the key didn't feel malevolent like the large cages, just magical.

"That's the one," purred the *Cait Sith*.

I unlocked her cage with a click, and she leapt lightly to the ground, sending the cage swinging back on its chain.

"Should I unlock the others?"

She licked her paw with disinterest. "I'm sure the birds would appreciate it, but I'd leave the badger alone if I were you. Avoid touching the larger cages, however. Unless you want to have a long nap and forget your parents forever."

I shuddered and unlocked the cage holding the two birds. They swooped from the cage and out the back window.

"Where's the key to the gate?" I whispered.

"In the parlor, behind the painting of the horned man."

I glanced in the direction of Gavin and Bronach's voices.

"That's right." She continued to groom herself. "By the front door. Best be quick about it."

I spared another glance at the cat on my way out, but she'd disappeared. Out the window, I guessed.

Creeping back through the house, I could hear Gavin explaining something about the last children's ages, and how some unseelie lord was unhappy. It was all rather icky, and I desperately hoped he was making it up.

The witch stood with her back to me. I'd expected an old crone from a fairy tale, but she looked young, with shining waves of white-gold hair tumbling down her back. I moved as quietly as I could, clutching the cloak around me. The painting hung above the mantle, a cruel-looking man with antlers sprouting from his brow. I eased it far enough away from the wall to see that the *Cait Sith* had been telling the truth. I unhooked the leather pouch that hung from the back of the painting. A quick peek inside revealed a golden band, big enough to slide up my arm, and a rolled piece of parchment.

I carefully slid the painting back into place and pocketed the pouch, preparing to creep toward the back door when a familiar voice made my blood run cold.

"Bronach," said Dylan cheerfully from the front door. "You look lovely as always."

No, no, no! How had he found us here?

I slowly turned to the doorway where my psychotic ex-boyfriend stood with his arm slung around Gavin's shoulder. Gavin was rigid with nerves but still looking at the witch, trying not to give away my presence in the parlor.

"Two wolves in one day." The witch sounded amused. "This is an occasion. Don't tell me Moriath has a second message for me."

"I highly doubt she even sent a first one. I've been looking for Gavin here all day. He's a wanted wolf, you know."

"Oh really? And what's a rogue wolf doing on my doorstep?"

"Distracting you, of course."

I stepped backward, my heart stuttering.

"You should be more careful, Bronach. And keep a better eye on your things. I think there's a thief in your living room."

Dylan's blue eyes scanned the room casually, then locked with mine.

"There you are, little girl."

CHAPTER 12

BEFORE DYLAN FINISHED SPEAKING, I RAN.

I could hear struggling at the doorway as Gavin wrestled Dylan, but I continued to sprint into the kitchen, climbing back through the open window, and half falling out of the cabin in my haste.

While I dashed across the clearing toward the trees, the witch yelled something after me in a language I didn't understand. Her words boomed and echoed around me, like thunder in a valley, the syllables all harsh edges and scraping sounds.

I hoped Gavin was on his way, but I didn't dare slow down to look. My foot caught on a root and I tripped, falling to the soft earth. To my horror, the root wrapped around my ankle. More roots crawled across the ground toward me as I frantically kicked to free myself.

"Audrey!" Gavin tumbled to the ground beside me and wrenched my foot free. He pulled me to my feet and into a run before I could register what had happened. He kept hold of my hand, dragging me to the trees as I stumbled and jumped to keep up with his long legs.

We slowed once we reached the cover of the forest. It was impossible to dash headlong through the trees and scratchy low bushes. My breath came in sharp gasps as we fled deeper into the woods.

"How did he know we were here?" I panted. We'd traveled for three days to get right back into the same position as before. Only, we also had a cranky witch after us now.

"Kylian must have sent him for me." Gavin didn't sound nearly as out of breath as I was. Stupid wolf.

"The Huntsman? Okay, then how does he know where we are?"

"He knows where all the wolves are." Gavin let go of my hand and slowed, looking around to see if anyone followed us. The forest was still. Maybe they hadn't bothered to chase us into the woods? "I was hoping he would be too busy to deal with me right away."

I leaned back against a tree, panting. "He knows? With…magic?"

"The tattoos. They contain a tracking spell."
Oh. Great.

"The ones on your arm? You didn't think that was useful information for me?"

"Not those. The other one." And with that, he stripped off his long-sleeved gray shirt.

Now, please remember, we had only dated for two months. In the winter. Shirts had never come off in that time. My frantic brain stuttered. It took me a moment or two to get over the abs…and the abs. And also, all the other muscles.

Gavin was still talking, tapping the tattoo over his heart. Oh right, tattoos.

"Um, if it's a tattoo, can't you just…get it removed? Or maybe damage the skin? How does it work?"

"No, it goes right through to the other side."

"Straight through…"

"My heart. That's why it's on the back too."

"It's on the back?" I pulled him around. Sure enough, a matching tattoo was inked on his back.

"Right, that's what I was saying. It's the same as Dylan's. All the wolves have them."

"How would I know that? I've never seen him without his shirt on." I ran my hand lightly over the tattoo on his shoulder blade and felt him shudder.

"You don't have to lie to me, Audrey."

My hand stilled on his back. "What do you mean?"

"Dylan told us. He couldn't stop bragging about it."

"What?!" I grabbed Gavin's arm and hauled him back around to face me. "What did he say about me?"

Gavin pulled his shirt back over his head, avoiding my penetrating glare. "About everything you did to-gether…"

"About how we had coffee? About how I tried to teach him to play Warcraft? Spit it out, Gavin!" By this point, I was probably being louder than was wise but I couldn't believe what he was implying.

"That you slept with him!" roared Gavin, finally looking me in the eyes. His dark gaze burned with rage, but it was no match for the fire I felt.

I inhaled deeply and glanced around. We couldn't be yelling right now. It was a miracle no one had found us yet. We needed to get moving again.

But first...

"Dylan told you that we slept together," I said flatly.

"He told us everything."

"That we had sex." I was doing my best to keep it together.

"And let me tell you, it was a bit of a shock after the way you told me I wasn't —how did you put it? —'getting into your pants' before I'd even kissed you."

I balled up my fist and punched him in the arm as hard as I could. I was sure he barely felt it, but it was the only way I could think of to get him to stop talking and actually listen to me. While he rubbed his arm, I tried to collect my thoughts. To be honest, I'd pretty much for-given him for breaking up with me. It was still painful to think about, but I knew he'd only been trying to keep me safe.

And I deserved Gavin's anger for dating Dylan. That had been really stupid. I should probably apologize. But now this?

"Why did you believe him?" I did my best to keep my voice low.

"What?"

"You might have been lying to me about who you really were, but I bared my heart to you. I told you *every-thing*. I thought no one knew me like you did. Yet you be-lieved I would do something like that?" *Quiet voice. Quiet voice.* I glanced through the trees. Nothing. We must have lost Dylan. "You thought I would sleep with some idiot boy that I didn't even like?"

"You never..."

"Never. Ever. Do you need it in writing?" I spun and started walking again, even though I had no idea where we were going. "We shouldn't stay here."

Gavin jogged a step to catch up with me, snagging my hand and tugging it gently. I reluctantly turned back to look at him.

"I'm sorry, Audrey." The pain in his dark eyes cut through me. "You're right, I never should have believed him. It's just...after I saw you kiss him..." He looked away and ran a hand through his messy hair.

I sighed, the anger draining from me. What a mess we were. "I'm sorry too. That was the stupidest thing I've ever done."

"Why did you do it?" Gavin tugged me closer, our toes close enough to touch. He pulled free a bit of my hair trapped under the collar of my cloak and ran it through his fingers. "Why did you kiss him? Agree to go out with him?"

I bit my lip and tried to put words to the heartache I'd been feeling that day. "I was going to tell him to get lost. I just wanted to be left alone. But then when I looked at you, and...it looked like you didn't even care."

"Oh, Audrey," he breathed and he pulled me in. I rested my head on his chest, listening to his heartbeat. "Dylan was testing me, to see how I'd react. If I'd told you to stay away from him, it would have shown how jealous I was. It would have undone everything I'd done to convince him you weren't important enough to toy with. I thought you'd walk away. I never expected that you'd kiss him."

Defying expectations. That was me.

"I didn't want to be with him. I just wanted to make you pay attention. I was so frustrated, and...I just wanted you to see me." Dang it, now I was crying. I pulled back, annoyed with myself.

"Audrey." Gavin wiped a tear from my cheek. "I've always seen you. Ever since that first day in History class, I've seen you. I haven't been able to look away. Forgive me for doubting you."

All the walls I had built up around my heart crumbled. I was so tired of fighting. I slid my arms around his neck and pressed my cheek against his to whisper into his ear, "Only if you forgive me for being so stupid."

Gavin's breath caught as I brushed my lips across the short hair at his temple, then along his cheek bone. His eyes fluttered closed, his hands settling on my hips.

My lips found his like it was the most natural thing in the world. Like we'd never been apart. Like I was coming home.

My heart pounded. He nipped my lip, then deepened the kiss. I shuddered when his tongue met mine.

I'd missed him. So much more than I'd ever admitted, even to myself.

A branch snapped.

Gavin immediately shoved me away from him, so hard I stumbled backward.

"Run!" he yelled as an enormous man appeared behind him. I caught an impression of dark skin and long swinging braids as the man yanked Gavin back and brought a dagger to his throat, the silver blade matching the axe strapped to the man's back. The Huntsman.

"Gavin!" I lunged for him, not caring what my odds were. Maybe I could distract the Huntsman so we could escape again.

Before I could take more than a step I was yanked backward, both my arms caught in an iron grip. I panicked, twisting in vain to see my captor. It must be Dylan.

But as a swirling gray mist rose around me, blocking the men and the forest from view, it was a woman's voice who whispered in my ear.

"Come, child. You can't save him."

CHAPTER 13

DATING DYLAN HADN'T ONLY BEEN THE stupidest thing I'd ever done, but also the most boring. No one had ever warned me that petty revenge could be so very dull. I'd only agreed to go out with the blond Irish exchange student to get a rise out of Gavin. I hadn't known that bad blood existed between the two of them, but apparently Dylan had only asked me out to annoy Gavin.

A mutual desire to antagonize someone else wasn't much to build a relationship on.

We didn't have anything in common, and honestly, I didn't try very hard to learn more about Dylan. He came over to my house once after school, and I tried to teach him how to play computer games.

After, he leaned in to kiss me, and I had pulled back. I just couldn't do it. Something had flickered in his gaze that made me wonder if he was going to force the issue. If I'd made a very dangerous choice with him. But then he'd simply laughed, told me I wasn't much fun, and left.

I should have ended it then, but that would have meant admitting I'd made a mistake. Pride wasn't any prettier than revenge, but there you have it. There were only four more weeks of school. Surely I could pretend for that long. So, I let Dylan take my hand whenever Gavin wandered past, let him play with my hair.

It was all a waste of time. Gavin didn't so much as look in our direction. It seemed that he was completely uninterested in what I did or who I was with. Every time he ignored me, my heart squeezed painfully in my chest. And so, I built those walls around it. I told myself that if he didn't care, I didn't care either.

I avoided any more time alone with Dylan, and we hung out once or twice at Neve's cafe where she watched him with narrowed eyes. I hadn't been able to bring myself to explain the whole stupid thing to her, but she had good instincts. She would casually remind me that she knew how to use a sword, thanks to years of fencing and HEMA (Historical European Martial Arts, for those who like it spelled out). I assured her that no stabbing was needed.

I hoped I was right.

Once school ended, and we had both officially graduated, I tried to break up with Dylan. It was difficult to do when he kept ignoring my texts. I supposed he would go back to Ireland soon anyway. But I wanted to tell him to his face that this thing between us was over. He totally ghosted me. Not even the promise of Neve's apple ginger pie was enough to make him appear.

I thought he was just bored of me. I never would have guessed he was actually super busy being a minion for an evil fae queen.

When the mist cleared, the forest, Gavin, and the Huntsman were gone. I stood in another clearing, this one home to a ruin that appeared to be the base of a tower. The weathered remains of an ornate stone arch and a ring of tumbled rock covered with moss and mushrooms were all that was left.

I stood there, stunned, as the hands holding my arms let go and a tall, olive-skinned woman stepped around to face me. Tucked behind pointed ears, her raven black hair hung straight to her knees, and her red silk gown swished as she moved, trailing on the mossy ground behind her.

"Where am I? I have to go back! I have to help Gavin!" The words tumbled out of me, tripping over each other in my urgency to be understood.

"I rescued you, to return your favor, you ungrateful human child." She punctuated her last word with a sharp tap of a long fingernail to my forehead.

"Ouch! What are you talking about? We've never met."

"Humans." The woman rolled her eyes. "You released me from my cage not fifteen minutes ago."

"What?!" I peered at the woman's eyes, a golden hue and slitted like a cat's. Like the cat from the witch's cottage. "But…"

"I told you, child, I'm a *Cait Sith*."

"My name is Audrey, and again, what?"

"A *Cait Sith*, and you may call me Liadan." The woman snapped her fingers as she walked toward the ruined tower. The rocks strewn about the clearing quivered. At first, I thought it was my imagination, but as she strode up to the arched doorway, they started to roll toward the ruin, losing their moss and mushrooms as they came. The tower built itself from the ground up, growing higher and higher as the stones rolled and leaped into place. Arched windows matching the door appeared, and a small stone balcony formed on the tower's side, stone by stone.

"Are you coming?" The *Cait Sith*, standing in the archway, interrupted my gawking. The final stones rolled up into place, creating a peaked roof of slate tiles. She disappeared into the dark tower.

I stood for a moment, stupefied. Then, after a quick look around the unfamiliar forest, I jogged after her.

The woman began to climb curved stone steps, a ball of flaming light hovering by her shoulder.

"Um, what is a *Cait Sith*?" I scrambled after Liadan, not wanting to be left behind when the light seemed to be traveling with her.

"You really know nothing," she said with careless disdain. "The *Cait Sith* are a race of fae. Among our talents is the ability to shift between our cat form and fae form."

"You mean, you can turn into a cat? Whenever you like?" That sounded handier than Gavin's forced nightly transformation.

"Nine times. Nine times we can transform. If we become a cat a tenth time, we lose our fae form forever."

Well, that was less handy.

"Why did the witch capture you? Did she know what you were?"

"That, human child, is not your business."

"Audrey," I reminded her.

She sniffed, stepping into a warmly lit room at the top of the stairs. I climbed up after her and looked around. The round room held a fireplace, already lit. Perhaps this shouldn't have been surprising in a tower assembled by magic. Liadan hung a kettle over the fire beside a bubbling cauldron. It smelled like dinner. Perhaps the *Cait Sith* equivalent of a crock pot?

The room had two arched windows with diamond panes of glass, but no balcony. That must be attached to the room above us. The stairs continued to climb up the curved wall and disappeared into a hole in the ceiling. The *Cait Sith* sat on a velvet upholstered chair next to a dark wooden table and motioned for me to join her. A matching chair slid out from the table, waiting.

I swallowed and sat. I'd seen bits and pieces of magic up to this point, but this room swam with it in golden floating motes. Liadan threw magic around without a care. I hoped I'd made the right choice in trusting her.

"I really need to get back to Gavin."

"So you said." The *Cait Sith* examined her long fingernails. "I assume you mean the wolf."

That's what the witch had said as well. "How can everyone tell he's a wolf? I dated him for two months and thought he was a human that whole time."

"Humans are terribly unobservant. Now, why do you want to help the wolf? Wolves can't be trusted. You do realize he's a pet of the Unseelie Queen."

"I know. He explained everything. But he's not like the others."

Liadan snorted. "So he's told you, I'm sure."

"I'm serious. He's saved my life more than once. He would never betray me."

The *Cait Sith* watched me, her cat eyes narrowed. "You're in love with him."

"I didn't say that!"

"You didn't have to. It's written across your face." She steepled her long fingers, thinking. "A human child in love with a wolf. It seems like a doomed arrangement. You're sure you don't want to go home? You can, you know. You have Bronach's key."

I'd forgotten about the key in all that had happened after stealing it. I pulled the leather bag from my pocket and tipped its contents onto the table. A piece of parchment tied with a leather cord, the gold bracelet, and a spill of tiny diamonds. I guessed diamonds were a universal currency. I hadn't set out to be a jewel thief, but I certainly wasn't going to return them.

"This is the key?" I picked up the bracelet. It hummed lightly in my hands, with more of those glowing patterns I was starting to expect with magical objects.

"It is. It was a gift from the Unseelie Queen to her sister. It will unlock any unseelie gate in Faerie or in your world."

"Are there many?"

"Unroll the parchment."

I did, using the bracelet to hold the edge down as I stretched it flat on the table. The page was a map. I guessed it must be *Tír na nÓg*—the mountains and coastline looked vaguely similar to the rough map Gavin had drawn in the dirt. It showed castles and creatures, all outlined in black, but glowing gold against them were a handful of stars, pulsing on the page.

"These are all the gates?" I counted thirteen of them. Most were in the northern section Gavin had said was the unseelie kingdom, but two stars twinkled in the south. Did the seelie fae know about them?

"All the unseelie gates," she said. "Now turn it over."

I flipped the parchment. On this side was a map of my world. It had hundreds of stars scattered over all the continents. I shivered, thinking of all the empty cages in the witch's cottage. I hoped stealing the key and the map would make life difficult for her.

"You see, child, you are currently here." She leaned forward and flipped the map back to the Faerie side, tapping a long fingernail against the parchment. A ruined tower on a small island. With a glowing star.

"You have a gate," I breathed.

"I do. When I choose to. I can travel home at will, but going out is easier with a gate. And you have the map, which allows you to visualize a gate you have never seen before, and the key to open any that may be locked, as mine is. I'd let you through regardless. After all, you saved me, and I repay my debts."

Liadan owed me for more than just setting her free from the cage. If I had the key, she didn't have to worry about Bronach showing up at her doorstep unannounced.

"And Gavin?" I examined the map of *Tír na nÓg.* "Do you know where the Huntsman would have taken him?"

"Yes, foolish child. There's only one place he would be." She tapped a star in the heart of the unseelie lands. "If you insist on going after him, you'll need to go through the Ice Gate, to Skyretaine Castle and the Unseelie Court."

CHAPTER 14

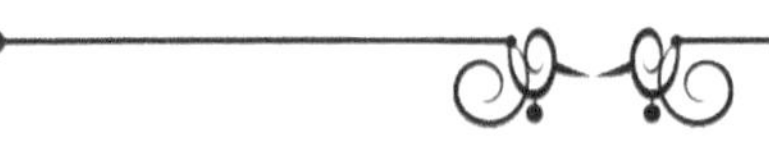

I JUMPED TO MY FEET. "THEN I NEED to get going! Where's your gate?"

"By all means, take off immediately and get killed along with your wolf." Liadan stood as well and strode over to a shelf lined with jars of dried plants.

"What?! Are they going to kill him?"

"One presumes." She opened a jar, sniffed it, then put it back on the shelf.

"Then I need to go get him right away! Thank you for your help." I needed to get moving. The enormity of my task would overwhelm me if I stopped to rest and think about it.

The *Cait Sith* opened another jar. This one seemed to meet with her approval, and she brought it back to the table.

"What do you know about magic, child?"

"I'm a level fifty-two mage in World of Warcraft."

"Pardon me?" She measured out two scoops from her jar into a small sieve.

"Nothing." I sighed. "I know nothing."

"So, if by some enormous stroke of luck you do manage to free the wolf from Moriath's kennels, then what? How long until the Huntsman finds you both again?"

I couldn't think of anything to say to that. I thumped back down into my chair.

"You should go home." She leaned over and tapped the gold bracelet, causing glowing patterns to jump off it. "Even if you could spellcraft, your chances would be slim. Without that skill, you walk into certain death."

"Is that what those glowing patterns on it are? The spell?"

Liadan stilled. "What do you see?"

I picked up the golden band and focused on the humming sensation, the patterns.

"It's like...a language I don't understand. At first, I thought I was imagining it, but it keeps happening. I see patterns made of light. Chains of interlocking symbols turning and twisting when I look at them too closely.

Sometimes I get a sensation from them." I shivered, remembering Bronach's cages.

"Hmm." Liadan tapped her long fingernails against the table. "You have the sight, then. That's uncommon in a faerie, but in a human? I've never heard of such a thing." She thought for a moment, narrowing her eyes at me. "Perhaps something can be done after all. Rest here tonight. Eat something. And perhaps I can teach you how the spell on your wolf's heart works." She opened a cupboard and took out a small china teapot.

"You said they'll kill him," I whispered.

"Not right away." The *Cait Sith* almost sounded kind. "Moriath is travelling in the north. Nothing will happen until she returns. You have time." She wrapped a trailing silk sleeve around her hand and unhooked the steaming kettle from over the fire.

I couldn't speak. Tears welled up in my eyes, blurring my vision.

"This will help." She poured water over the sieve into the teapot. A strong herbal scent drifted up from it.

I sniffled. "Is it magic?"

"It's even better." She set two thin china teacups next to the teapot. "It's peppermint tea."

She was right. Without disabling the tracking spell, we'd never get away from the Huntsman. I supposed I needed to trust her—even if she thought tea was a solution to anything.

I survived the tea and ate a bowl of deliciously woodsy mushroom soup and a fresh bun from the magical fireplace. Then the *Cait Sith* took me upstairs where I bathed in a steaming tub with neither taps nor a drain. When I finished my bath, I was nearly dead on my feet. Liadan lent me a nightgown that pooled on the floor when I pulled it over my head, and I slipped into her silk canopied bed where I fell asleep almost before my eyes closed.

I woke up in a startled panic, falling out of bed in a heap of silk quilts and tangled nightgown. It was dark outside, the moon shining in through the diamond-paned glass door that led to the balcony. How long had I slept? What if I was too late? I fumbled for my glasses and found my cloak at the foot of the bed, swinging it on as I raced down the stairs.

Liadan sat at the table, the surface covered with papers and dripping candles. She looked up and raised an eyebrow mildly.

"How long was I asleep?" I gasped.

"Not long enough by the looks of you." Liadan gestured at a chair, which obligingly pulled itself out from the table. "Sit, child. I've been looking into the tracking spell on the wolves."

I sat.

"Tea?"

"Coffee?" I pleaded.

"Hmmm?"

Wait, did they not have coffee in this realm? I shuddered. I needed to rescue Gavin and get home. And quickly.

"Fine. Yes, tea."

She poured me a cup and I sipped the insipid liquid while I listened, my racing heart calming.

"First of all, it helps if you understand how magic works in Faerie. There are two main ways in which magic can be used. There is small magic. Healing, preserving…"

"Moving chairs?"

"Precisely. These are accomplished through the use of the natural magic of Faerie. They are limited to how effectively the faerie can utilize their surroundings."

"Like…chakra?"

She blinked.

"The force?"

"And then," she continued, ignoring my nonsense, "there are magical objects. A skilled faerie with the sight can spellcraft. They can infuse objects with magic that can be used by anyone. The gates are an example of this. And your cloak."

I fingered the golden embroidered edge of my cloak, feeling again the hum of magic emanating from it.

"Magical objects are nearly always metal. They hold the spell better. Gold—and occasionally jewels—for most objects of power, silver for weapons, iron for...less appealing spells. The spell infusing the metal is basically a list of commands. Depending on what is asked of them, they respond in the manner the creator wishes, even without the creator there. Even seemingly simple spells, like your cloak's ability to distort the viewer's perception of the wearer, is actually a complicated list of possible commands. Questions and answers."

I thought about this. Then...

"It's like code!"

The *Cait Sith* gave a feline tilt of her head.

"Um, okay, so in the human world, our technology —computers and phones—work in a similar way, I think. The programmer, the creator of the program, writes a list of commands, ways to respond to the user's input."

She blinked. "I'm not familiar with the spells of your realm, but it would make sense for them to follow similar rules."

"Okay, so how does that help Gavin?"

"The oath Moriath has the wolves swear, the power from it, is bound into their tattoos. The ink for the tattoos is a solution of powdered gold. It binds the spell through the heart and cannot be broken without the oath-magic rebounding on the wearer. Killing them."

"Then...there's nothing we can do?" Despair washed over me.

"I didn't say that. I said that the spell can't be broken. But I believe I can teach you how to disrupt it, to change the list of commands. At least for a time."

"You mean…" A smile stretched across my face as I felt actual hope for the first time since Gavin had been taken. "It can be hacked! Show me."

CHAPTER 15

THE SUN SHONE INTO THE CLEARING FROM high above as I stood with Liadan in front of her tower. We had spent hours talking over the basics of the patterns that made up faerie spells. Then Liadan had shown me how to disable the spell on my cloak and fix it again.

When I asked her if it was as good as new, Liadan had given me a liquid shrug and said, "Close enough."

I was wrapped in it now, over a borrowed dress of purple silk. The gown had been much too big when I tried it on, but Liadan had simply waved her hand, and it had shrunk to fit like it had been tailored for me. I still wore my red chucks, though. There was no way I'd leave my favorite shoes in Faerie, and besides, they were far more

comfortable than the tall, heeled boots the *Cait Sith* pre-
ferred.

"I do wish you'd take off those ridiculous specta-
cles." Liadan sniffed. "If anyone looks too closely, they
might notice. The *Tuatha Dé Danann* are never near-
sighted."

"How lovely for them." I adjusted my glasses self-
consciously. "But, as I'm pretty much blind without them,
I think I'll risk it. Anyway, the cloak should make it so no
one can see them anyway, right?"

She just blinked at me, and I sighed. So reassuring.

I glanced around the clearing, empty except for
the tower. "Where's the gate?"

The *Cait Sith* gave me an amused, half smile and
sidelong look as she snapped her fingers. The clearing
rumbled, then the tower began to collapse in on itself. The
stones crashed and rolled to the ground, many gaining
moss and mushrooms as they settled back onto the forest
floor. But the arched door remained, humming with magical energy.

"Ooooh," I breathed.

"Off you go, human child. Good luck on your en-
deavor." She examined her nails, not showing any emotion
on her face. "Should you survive, feel free to use that key
to return through the Ruined Gate and tell me your story
over a cup of peppermint tea. I've unlocked it for your
use."

I smiled at her. "Oh, I will. But I'll bring the drinks, thanks. Wait till you try an americano."

The *Cait Sith* merely raised an elegant eyebrow, and I walked to the gate. Standing in front of the arched doorway, I held the golden bracelet in one hand and pictured the glowing star on the map. With a deep breath, I stepped through.

In the time it took me to blink, I stood on a platform staring at a towering castle of ice. Sharp spires cut toward the sky as fat snowflakes drifted down from the clouds. Skyretaine.

The platform I'd come out on was high above the ground, with stairs of carved ice gracefully curving downward. I glanced back at the gate I'd just come through and yelped.

The gate itself was made of sparkling ice that matched the castle. It twisted and curved in a way that was both artistic and organic. But just beyond the gate, a few inches from my toes, the ground fell away in a dizzying drop. I put out a hand to steady myself against the Ice Gate and felt the soft hum of magic. A small part of my brain felt *through* the buzzing to catch a glimpse of the magical code that made the gate work. It was ancient and intricate.

The rest of my brain was freaking out. I breathed deeply, fixing my eyes on the village rooftops and autumn forest below me, so far down that they looked like a miniature world. I stepped back carefully, aware that I needed to put some distance between myself and the gate. Even if my cloak still worked, I shouldn't be standing in a gate that was supposed to be locked.

I'd explained to Liadan what Gavin had said about the wolves busily chasing Isobel—who'd hopefully evaded them. With them so distracted, she'd felt it was the best possible time for me to stage a jailbreak. If the Queen still traveled in the north, and the Huntsman and wolves were busy in the human world, then the castle should be relatively empty. The unseelie courtiers avoided Skyretaine and its unpredictable mistress as much as they could manage.

The *Cait Sith* had been right. The place looked deserted. Even the front door was unguarded. The massive double doors had an icy dragon carved into its archway, with folded wings and a fierce, horned head. Tucked around it, smaller winged and furred creatures were carved into the ice. The work was so intricate that I reached out to touch the wing of a small creature that reminded me of a gargoyle.

It stirred under my hand.

I gulped and stepped back. Would the cloak work on magical carvings? The little gargoyle blinked sleepily at me, and I tried to think unseelie thoughts. Ice ...wolves...child-stealing witches...I was no good at this.

The gargoyle tucked its nose under its carved wing and went still again.

I let out the breath I'd been holding, then turned and walked briskly along the side of the castle, trying to look like I belonged there in case anyone saw me. Liadan had said that with my cloak, I should pass well enough for a high fae, and that the small folk of the castle wouldn't question me. Probably.

I pulled out a piece of parchment from my dress's pocket—the rough map Liadan had drawn for me before I left. When I'd asked her how she knew it so well, the *Cait Sith* had merely sniffed. Not my business, apparently.

According to her sketch, I could access the kennels from the outside. I followed her arrows along the exterior of the castle, past graceful towers and windows patterned with swirling frost. Skyretaine was more beautiful than I'd expected the home of an evil faerie queen to be.

I passed the occasional servant, and it was all I could do not to stop and stare at the faeries. Some had skin like stone, while others had curving horns or lashing tails. All kept their heads down as I boldly strode past.

At last, I came to what must be the kennels. Stone steps led down to a pair of gray, wooden doors. Wolves carved in ice slept on either side of the doorway. The tail of one flicked as I reached for the iron handle, but they seemed content to let me in. I could only hope they would also let us back out.

I peeked first, then slipped into an empty room full of comfortable chairs and couches, with large stone fireplaces on either wall. I tiptoed across the thick rug toward an open doorway to the next room. Peering around the doorframe, I glimpsed a long dormitory full of bunks and storage chests. All empty. But at the very end, I could see Gavin sitting in a barred cell.

Something unknotted in my chest at the sight of him. Still alive. I'd been terrified that for all Liadan's logic, I would arrive too late.

But Liadan had been right again. Apparently, the Huntsman often disciplined the wolves with a night in the cell if they caused too much trouble. Again, how did she know so much about the Unseelie Court?

After a moment, Gavin noticed me. His eyes flicked over to me in surprise, but then he quickly looked away, not wanting to reveal my position to his jailer.

Dylan. Of course it was him. My least favorite person lounged on the bunk closest to the cell, twirling a set of keys. I pulled back into the sitting room and glanced around for anything that might work as a weapon. I heard Gavin's voice from the other room, too quiet for me to make out his words.

From Dylan's seething reaction, my wolf must be trying to pick a fight to keep his attention off me. I settled on an iron poker—blessedly magicless—hanging next to a fireplace. It wasn't as cool as a sword or anything, but unlike Neve, I wouldn't know what to do with one anyway.

Poker in hand, I crept through the door. The alpha had his back to me as he growled at Gavin.

I was nearly to them when my sneaker squeaked against the stone tiles. Gavin winced and his tanned skin blanched as Dylan spun to face me.

CHAPTER 16

LOOK WHO IT IS!" MY EVIL ex-boyfriend grinned. "Audrey, sweetheart, how are you? I've been missing you. I was so sad when I lost you at the Lichen Gate, but here you are."

"Dylan, you idiot. Unlock the cell." I kept the poker out of sight under the folds of my cloak.

He smirked, obviously not threatened by my human self. "Come here and give me a kiss, and I'll think about it."

A laugh burst out of me, and he looked puzzled.

"Okay, now I know this cloak is working."

"What?"

"My cloak? It makes the viewer—that's you, by the way—see what they expect to see."

"What are you talking about? I know about the cloak. I can see you."

Gavin leaned against the bars of his cell with a lazy smile while he watched me.

"Well, dummy, you clearly expect to see a silly, weak little girl." I smiled sweetly at him. "Or else you'd be more afraid right now."

And with that, I swung the poker straight at his smug, stupid face.

Dylan swore as he stumbled back against the cell bars, blood dripping down his face. Gavin's arm snapped out from the cell and caught Dylan neatly around the neck.

The blond wolf's face reddened as he struggled to free himself from the iron grip. No such luck.

"Still want that kiss?" I asked him. His death glare said probably not, but sadly, he lost consciousness before he could respond.

I plucked the gold key from the stone tiles and unlocked the cell door. Gavin let an unconscious Dylan slide to the ground and stepped through. He caught me in a strong hug, and I released a shaky breath.

He felt so solid with his arms around me. My wolf.

"You came for me," he murmured into my hair. "I saw you disappear with that woman and I thought I'd never see you again."

"She rescued me." I allowed myself to relax against his chest. "So that I could rescue you. I suppose we both owe her one." I sighed, reluctantly pulling back. "We should do something about Dylan."

We decided to deposit the alpha in the locked cell. I hoped he would have the worst headache of his life when he woke up. Gavin snagged a leather backpack from a chest, tossing a couple of items into it before slinging it over his shoulder.

"Captain Prepared," I teased. He gave me a crooked smile before grabbing my hand and dashing for the door.

"Wait!" I pulled him to a stop.

"I assume you got here with the witch's key?"

"Yes." I showed him my wrist with the humming gold bracelet. "And her map. But if we leave now, Kylian will just track you down again."

Gavin sighed and ran a hand through his hair. "I know, but the best we can do is get a head start. I'll drop you off at home where you'll be safe."

I ignored that last bit and tugged him toward the sitting room couches.

"Take off your shirt."

"So forward." Gavin laughed. "You're not getting into my pants, you know."

"Oh, shut up and sit down. Let me take a look at your tracking spell."

He looked at me curiously but did as I asked. A shirtless Gavin was very distracting, and I closed my eyes for strength.

"Audrey?"

"Just a second." I took a deep breath and focused on the tattoo. I placed my hand over it, feeling the beat of Gavin's heart against my palm. Closing my eyes again, I reached for the magic's pattern, unspooling like chains of code in my mind. "Okay, so it looks like the tracking spell is entangled with your transformation spell. Hopefully I can disrupt them both and keep you from turning furry at sunset. They're connected to an anchor of some sort. Do you think we could steal it?"

"It's tattooed around Kylian's bicep, so that would be tricky. How can you tell?"

I glanced up at him. "When you were captured, I was saved by Liadan, a *Cait Sith* I rescued from the witch. That's who you saw me disappear with. She showed me how to understand magical spells."

Gavin covered my hand with his. "That's not a common skill, not by a long shot. I don't feel anything when I touch the tattoo beyond a faint magical humming."

"She was surprised, too," I said. "I guess I have the sight, whatever that means."

I paused for a moment to enjoy the warmth of Gavin's hand over mine, then closed my eyes and went back to examining the spell.

"There's also what I'm guessing is a compulsion spell. Two users." I opened my eyes. "Moriath and Kylian, right?"

Gavin nodded, his eyes wide.

"Kylian didn't order you to stay here?" I asked, dropping my hand into my lap.

Gavin narrowed his eyes. "No. I suppose he thought the cell would be enough. He sure didn't see you coming."

"Hmm, I do like to keep things interesting. Now shush. I need to concentrate."

He bit his lip. "Yes ma'am."

This boy would be the death of me.

I shut my eyes and fought to regain my focus. The spell wasn't straight and orderly like code. It swirled and wandered and twined around itself. I pried the strands apart like Liadan had shown me and spun them together in nonsensical ways. It took some time to change the whole pattern, and I could feel how the spell was already working to crawl back into its old pattern. It was the best I could do.

I opened my eyes. The sitting room felt foreign at first, my brain still half in the world of spells. I shook my head.

"So, Spellcrafter, did you disable the spell?" Gavin asked.

"I prefer the term spell hacker, thank you very much. And I wasn't able to disable it permanently, but I did disrupt it for a bit."

"How long is a bit?" Gavin stood and pulled his long-sleeved gray shirt back on.

"About a week?" I rose too, flipping my hood back up.

He nodded. "That will give me a good start. Thank you, Audrey."

After all this, he was really planning to just up and leave me? A little rougher than necessary, I elbowed past him and opened the kennel's wooden door, leaning out to peek up the stairs.

"The place seemed pretty deserted on my way in," I told him in a low voice. "I didn't see any guards or any-thing."

"The other wolves are still in the human realm," murmured Gavin. "But that's not what I'm worried about. Stay calm."

He eased out the door, the picture of relaxation. Squeezing my hand, he pulled me behind him.

As we crept up the stairs, I couldn't help glancing back at the doorway to the wolves' kennel. The carved ice wolves beside the doors stirred. The one on the left stretched, flashing a toothy yawn. But the wolf on the right was staring right at us, its lips curled back in an icy snarl.

"Um...Gavin..." We were nearly at the top of the stairs now.

He looked back too and stiffened.

"Okay, forget calm," he whispered. "On three, we run for the gate. Ready?"

I nodded.

Both icy wolves watched us with bared fangs now.

"One." The wolf on the right shook one paw free of the icy castle wall and set it on the bottom step.

"Two." I gripped Gavin's hand tighter and gathered up my silk skirts in my other hand, preparing to run.

"Three!"

We bolted up the remaining steps in a blur of speed. Ice splintered behind us and as I surged up the last step behind Gavin. He pulled me along, running full speed along the castle wall. My scarlet cloak streaked behind me.

The scrabble of icy feet pounded behind us as we slid around the corner to face the main door.

The wolves let out a bone-chilling howl, and the carvings around the door fixed us with icy stares.

"Crap!" I yelped.

"Don't slow down!" Gavin pulled me toward the stairs leading up to the Ice Gate. I heard another splintering sound, only much, much louder than when the wolves broke free.

The dragon was awake.

My breath came in stabbing gasps. I'd always hated running in cold weather.

Why were there so many stairs? I scrambled up them as fast as I could.

"Okay, once we reach the gate, use the key and visualize your gate at Pilot Bay."

Thank you, Captain Obvious.

—Is what I would have said if I had any air available for witty retorts.

"Hopefully Kylian is too busy to worry about watching that gate now that I'm safely locked away."

I nodded breathlessly and glanced over my shoulder, then wished I hadn't. The wolves lunged onto the bottom stairs, the dragon looming not far behind them. It had to be as long as a city bus. Where was the little gargoyle?

"I'll drop you off and go. A week will give me a good head start. Thank you again, Audrey," Gavin said, finally sounding a bit winded as we reached the top of the steps.

"Are you kidding me right now?" I gasped.

"What do you mean—Whoa!" he yelled when I jerked backward, half strangled as my hood was yanked. Time slowed as I fell toward the icy steps and the magical predators surging upward.

Gavin lunged forward and caught my wrist, pulling me back onto the step. He used the momentum to slide past me and punch something. I spun to see a small winged shape tumble and smash against the closest wolf.

Oh, so that's where the gargoyle was.

Gavin and I stumbled to the gate, panting.

"Can we talk about our future plans when we don't have a giant ice dragon behind us?" I glared at him and grabbed his hand.

Icy claws scraped up the last stairs as we eyed the cliff on the other side of the gate.

"Ready?" he asked me.

"For anything." I squeezed his hand and together we jumped through the gate, leaping toward the sharp drop into thin air, and thinking of home.

CHAPTER 17

WE HIT THE GROUND IN THE DARK, stumbling into the forest outside of Pilot Bay. "It looks exactly the same as when we left." I kept Gavin's hand firmly in mine as I glanced around.

"It's probably only been a couple of hours," he said. "Time flows slower here, remember."

"Hmm, those ice things aren't going to come bursting through the gate, are they?" I turned and looked behind us. Sure enough, I could faintly see an arch where twining branches from two trees made a gate in the forest. It wouldn't look like much of anything if it weren't for the glowing bits of magic climbing up from the ground and through the trees. A magical artifact must have been buried to power the gate.

"They're tied to Skyretaine. They can't leave the castle grounds."

I sighed in relief, then realized something. It was night but…"You're not a wolf! My hack is working."

He kissed me on the cheek with his very human lips. "I never doubted it. Now come on, we should get you home. Your parents must be worried."

"They're away for the week." I held my ground and tightened my grip on his hand. "And if you think I'm just going home and letting you leave, then you haven't been paying attention."

Gavin reached for my other hand. "You've got your family here, and Neve. It's not going to be safe with me."

"Exactly! You've only got a week at most until your tracking spell restarts. You won't be safe without me. We go together."

"You'll give up your life here? College in the fall? For someone who's been lying to you since the day we met? You don't even know me. Not really."

"Well, now I know everything. Everything is different. Everything but you."

"Audrey—"

"No, you listen to me. You say you were lying to me, but ever since you left to find your brother, you've been lying to everyone. Including yourself. But you've always been yourself with me. You talk like you were pretending before, but the whole time we were in Faerie, you were still the same boy who teased me about my coffee addiction. The same boy who kissed me on the lookout this spring. You haven't been lying to me, not about who you are. Maybe I'm the only person you've been truly honest with."

Gavin stood silently, and I reached up to touch his face in the faint moonlight. I was surprised to feel tears on his cheek.

"Don't make me leave you," I whispered. "Not now that I finally have you back."

He leaned down and kissed me softly. His lips tasted salty with tears. "Okay."

"Okay?"

Gavin tucked my hair behind my ear. "Do you think I have the strength to push you away a second time? Doing it once was the most painful thing I've ever done. I'm not sure I'd survive leaving you again."

I sighed with relief and rested my hand on his chest, feeling his heart beating against my fingers. "Good, because on a less romantic note, I'm pretty sure Dylan isn't going to be too impressed with me, and he knows where I live."

Gavin stiffened. "And he knows where this gate is. We should get as far away as we can."

"We should," I agreed. I ran my fingers along the edge of the velvet cloak. "But there's someone I need to talk to first."

The lights still shone from the windows of Miss Chloe's cabin. We waited at the forest's edge as a woman waved goodbye and left in her truck.

"Come in, children," called Miss Chloe from the doorway. "Book club just ended, and I still have a couple of cupcakes that need eating."

Gavin looked at me. "The librarian?"

"I know, right?" I tugged him up the steps and we slipped off our shoes in the cozy entryway.

"Come sit, my dears." Miss Chloe waved us into the rose-covered living room. "You must be tired. All that running about."

I looked at her suspiciously. "What do you know about that?"

"Oh, I like to keep an eye on things." The older lady winked at me merrily. "My cloak seems to have gotten a lot of use."

I undid the clasp and pulled it off. The satin lining whispered against my skin, as if saying goodbye.

"I'm sorry it's a bit...dirty." I held it up with a wince. The plush crimson velvet was matted in places, the embroidered gold hem covered in mud.

"Hmm, yes." Miss Chloe took the cloak and shook it out. She coughed as a cloud of dust rose from it. "Nothing a good dry cleaning shouldn't solve. I best drop it off in the morning, I'll be needing it soon."

"Wasn't it for Neve?" I sat on the couch next to Gavin, pressing my leg against his through my purple silk skirts. How had Neve ended up with an adopted aunt who kept magical bits of clothing?

"Well, she may have need of it yet, but hopefully not this week." Miss Chloe folded up the dirty cloak and set it on the coffee table.

"Does Neve know about...all of this?" I waved vaguely at the cloak, but I meant more than that.

"Oh, no, my dear." Miss Chloe set a plate with two cupcakes on the table and Gavin snagged one. "And I'd appreciate it if you didn't tell her anything about your very interesting adventures. The less she knows, the safer she is. At least for now."

Gavin stilled next to me. "Neve's the lost unseelie crown princess." It wasn't a question.

Miss Chloe didn't acknowledge him. "And I'm sure you can guess this, but it's best if you leave Pilot Bay for a little while. Between the Huntsman and Bronach, you've attracted quite a bit of attention to yourselves. Where do you think you'll go?"

I pulled out the leather pouch and unrolled the map on the coffee table, human realm side up. I peered at the little gold stars in our part of the world.

"There are two unseelie gates by Pilot Bay?"

"Only one, in the old mine up the mountainside," said Miss Chloe.

"Then what's this one?" I tapped the second star.

"The one you traveled through, of course. I installed it last year. Seemed like it might come in handy. I call it the Wolf Gate." She winked at Gavin.

"I thought this map only showed the unseelie gates."

"It shows all the gates you have access to, and the Wolf Gate will be waiting for you when it's time for you to come home again."

I ran my finger over the star. Home. But not yet. "What do you think?" I nudged Gavin with my knee. "Look at all those stars to choose from. Where should we go first?"

He examined the map thoughtfully. "Let's talk about priorities." He looked up and gave me a crooked smile. "Where can we get you a good cup of coffee?"

See? I knew there was a reason I loved that boy.

EPILOGUE

"WHAT DID MY PARENTS SAY TO YOU?" I asked Neve on Facetime.

Gavin sat across the little cafe table from me, his gold plugs glinting in his deceptively human ears while he took his first bite of Parisian dessert.

His eyes closed momentarily in bliss and I laughed.

"I mean, they seem to believe you, that you're really at BCIT early for the super-special programming camp. Even though you've actually deferred enrollment to British Columbia's top tech school to run around Europe." Neve didn't sound impressed. I didn't blame her.

A week had passed since our jump through the Ice Gate. It'd been tough to convince Neve to help me with my parents without telling her the whole truth. Neve was my best friend, and I trusted her with my life, but I also trusted Miss Chloe's advice. And really, how was I supposed to explain magic portals and a boyfriend who turned into a wolf?

Was Gavin's guess correct? It was hard to believe my best friend could be a faerie princess, but I was starting to believe in a lot of things these days. Either way, we needed to stay far away from Pilot Bay.

Besides, I'd always wanted to see Paris. And next week, who knew?

The map still filled me with wonder. Little glowing stars lit up like the Milky Way across every continent. The unseelie fae had built a lot of gates over the millennia.

"Never mind your parents. There are more important things to discuss." Neve leaned in toward the screen. "What are you eating right now? I can't believe you're at *Ladurée*."

"Gavin is enjoying a *tarte aux framboises*. It's the closest he could get to a cheesecake, and it's apparently okay." I reversed the camera on my phone so Neve could see my wolf blissfully eating another bite.

"I'm gonna look that up after we finish chatting. Now, how about you?"

I turned the camera down at my own plate to show her the macarons. "Lavender with a lemon zest buttercream."

"Hmmm...I'm going to need photos and detailed notes of everything."

I laughed. "Deal. But Neve, it's barely worth mentioning the pastries. The coffee here. *The coffee*. I may have died and gone to heaven."

"Can you try to get to *Pierre Hermé* and order a *Montebello* while you're in Paris? Oh, and a *Helena,* and then tell me what the filling is like? I can't find a decent recipe in English. I really should have paid more attention in French class."

I promised I would, then we chatted for another few minutes about the cafe and her fencing lessons before saying our goodbyes.

"You'd better be worth all this," Neve told Gavin, with a world of threat in her voice. "And you better not be taking advantage of my friend, or I swear I will hunt you down and end you."

"I promise, my intentions are honorable," Gavin told her.

"Separate hotel rooms." Neve narrowed her eyes.

"Have you even met Audrey?"

"Neve, I know this is a lot, but you have to trust me." I blew her a kiss. "I'll call again tomorrow. I love you."

She signed off, and I sighed as I tapped my phone to end the call.

"Do you regret coming with me?" Gavin looked at me seriously over the decimated remains of his dessert.

"I can tell how much you miss Neve. And I don't like that you've put off school for a year."

"I'd have to leave Neve anyway in a month. And school can wait a year. I'm sure by then we'll have figured out a way to scramble the spell permanently. I just hate lying to her."

We left some money on the table and wandered out of the cafe. We'd exchanged one of the diamonds for euros, doubtless getting ripped off in the process, but we had money to live off of.

After wearing the velvet cloak day and night for so long, I felt a bit exposed on the busy sidewalk in my red hoodie and jean shorts, but no one paid any attention to us. In fact, we might as well have been invisible until Gavin collided with someone. The tall blond boy in a green t-shirt was obviously too enamored with his beautiful, curly-haired girlfriend to look where he was going.

"Sorry!" I called after them, even though I wasn't the one who'd run into someone. The Canadian in me was hard to repress.

We walked hand in hand to the low cement wall overlooking the Seine. Across the river stood the Eiffel Tower. I sighed. I still couldn't believe we were in Paris.

Gavin seemed less interested in the view. He boosted me up onto the cement wall, leaving his hands around my waist as he leaned in for a kiss. I felt him smile against my lips before he pulled back.

"Have I told you how much I love you?" He pressed his forehead to mine and I closed my eyes, perfectly content.

"Not today, you haven't."

"No?" he laughed.

"Not this week, actually." I leaned back and tapped my chin. "It's been...at least two months since you told me."

"Two months! Well, Audrey, I love you. And I love you at least twice as much as I did two months ago."

"Really?" I kicked my dangling feet, still in my trusty red chucks. "How much will you love me next month?"

"At least twice as much again." He kissed my temple and I shivered.

"And in ten years?" I held my breath.

He smiled. "I'm not sure I have the math skills to answer that question. Why don't you ask me every day until then, and we'll figure it out together?"

"It's a deal." I grinned up at him. "I love you, too, by the way."

"Oh, I know."

I rearranged myself on the wall to face the river.

"You know, we'll have to leave here soon." Gavin swung his long legs over and sat next to me. "Where are we headed to next?"

It was true. As perfect as Paris had been, we couldn't stay anywhere for too long. I pulled the map out of my pocket and we looked at all the twinkling stars. So many possibilities. I twined my fingers with Gavin's, knowing I would be just as content, anywhere in either realm, as long as we were together.

But that didn't mean I didn't have a bucket list. I tapped a star in the middle of the map.

"Have you ever heard of the pyramids?"

Want to find out if Isobel Watson escaped the wolves? Read The Rose Gate, a Retelling of Beauty and the Beast, available now!

THE WOLF GATE

Author's Note

My version of Tír na nÓg is loosely based on Irish folklore. If you'd like to learn more about the world and the faeries that inhabit it, go to my website where you can find a map and a list of the various races with a little bit about each of them.

At my website you can also see illustrations I drew for all the books, and sign up for my newsletter. I use my newsletter to send you updates on my books, peeks at upcoming art, and fun printables.

www.HannaSandvig.com

Acknowledgements

A BIG THANK YOU TO MY ALPHA READERS, my husband Craig and my dear friends Sonya and Julie. Your belief in my stories and support for my writing keeps me going.

Thanks to my incredible beta readers, Stephanie, Jessica, Kirstin, Tessonja, Clari, Patrizia, Laura, Merie, Sona, Colleen, Adlin, Mar, and Kari. You had a lot of opinions about this one, and your feedback made it so much better.

Thanks to my mom for your wonderful feedback, both on the manuscript and my publishing plans. I am so blessed to have you helping me on this author journey.

Thanks to Becky, you're an amazing editor and a great friend. I appreciate the heck out of you.

Thank you to Sarah for drawing the sweet illustration of Liadan's tower on the opposite page! You can check out her art on instagram: @hihappymail

Most of all, thank you to God. The world you created is so much more inspiring and magical than anything my human brain could write. I'm constantly amazed by your love.

The 1st Faerie Tale Romance

THE ROSE GATE

a Retelling of Beauty and the Beast

by

HANNA SANDVIG

CHAPTER 5

"THERE YOU GO, *ÀLAINN*," SAID A LOW gentle voice. I opened my eyes. A big beast of a man hovering over me. He had a brown, bushy beard, and his long hair had twigs stuck in it. It was his face, however, that was truly shocking. One gray eye stared into mine, but the other side of his face was sliced with old scars from top to bottom, his left eye completely gone. What had happened to him?

I lay on some sort of velvet couch as he tied a bandage around my injured arm that looked much cleaner than I would have expected given the ragged state of his dark clothes.

I shrank back from his touch and glanced wildly around me. Stone walls and gilded furniture were lit by sunshine pouring through the velvet-draped window. This was not the miner's cabin. And how long had I been unconscious? Why did my arm not hurt more? The wolf bite should have been throbbing, but it was just a dull ache.

The man reached toward my bandaged arm and I jumped, pulling back from the one-eyed monster.

He made a shushing noise, like you would to a crying baby or a skittish animal, but I was not shushed. I needed to get out of here.

"You see, my lord," said a raccoon, popping its head up beside the bed. "I told you to shave. You look terrifying."

I blinked at the raccoon. Nope, this was not okay.

"What sort of drugs did you give me?!" I shrieked at the beastly man, who drew back, looking startled. I kicked off the light blanket covering my legs and tumbled to the floor.

"No, I didn't give you anything, you don't understand!" The man reached for me, but I scrambled away from him and got to my feet.

"Where did you bring me?" My voice rose as I edged toward the door.

He started toward me and I didn't wait for an answer. I bolted for the door and swung myself out into the hallway. Whatever this place was, it was huge, but the massive stairway to my left seemed promising so I ran to it, my bare feet sinking into the thick rug that ran down the middle of the stone floor. I spun down the twisting stairwell. I had no time to waste, the one-eyed man looked about a foot and a half taller than me. He'd catch up to me quickly.

But I had terror on my side and stone stairs were much easier to navigate than a slippery path in the dark. My twisted ankle seemed completely healed and even the bite on my arm was more itchy than painful. How long had I been asleep?

I stumbled into a foyer and had a brief impression of gilded mirrors and glass lanterns before I pulled open the heavy oak doors. I paused and sneezed at the bright sunshine.

"Wait!" The man sounded close behind me.

Too close. Nope, not waiting. I yelped as my feet hit the gravel path at the bottom of the stairs. I ignored the sharp little rocks as I passed exuberant rose bushes edging the path. A high stone wall surrounded the garden, but at the end of the path, a stone arch covered by roses formed a perfectly circular gate. I could vaguely make out a dirt trail on the other side. It must be the way out.

"It's not safe!"

I glanced back and almost tripped at the sight of the grand stone castle behind me. How far from home was I? Surely, I would have heard if there were a castle anywhere near Pilot Bay? A question for another time. I needed to focus on escaping the crazed man behind me.

He had almost caught up to me now. "You need to wait until the sun comes up."

"It's daytime. What are you even talking about!?" I gasped, but I didn't wait for an answer. I dashed through the rose gate toward freedom.

And plunged into darkness.

My feet slid on the muddy path and my eyes strained to adjust to the sudden lack of sunlight. My shoulder smacked against a tree and I held onto it to keep myself from falling.

I was back in the forest where the wolves had been chasing me. I heard a soft snarl. The wolves were still chasing me.

It was as if the castle with the roses and the talking raccoon had been a vivid dream.

Which, given the talking raccoon, actually made a lot of sense.

My eyes adjusted to the dark just in time to see the wolf launch itself at me. Then a breathy snarl made me flinch to the side as the giant grizzly bear appeared behind me. The bear knocked the first wolf to the ground, but three more leapt onto him, teeth sinking into his shoulder and foreleg. I stumbled back a couple of steps and found myself blinking in the bright rose garden again.

What?

It had to be some sort of…portal? Magic doorway? I was back at the castle and the forest with the wolves was somehow on the other side. And so was that bear who had now saved my life twice. He'd been covered in wolves when I left. He was pretty big, but those odds didn't seem fair.

I spied an old pitchfork leaning against the garden wall. This was a terrible idea. I grabbed it anyway and jumped back through the arch of roses.

Darkness swallowed me again, but I swung the pitchfork with all my might at the wolf on the grizzly's shoulder, yelling at the top of my lungs. After all, she who hesitates is lost, right?

The wolf fell to the ground, dazed, and the bear and wolves all paused and stared at me in shock. Well, yes, I was surprised too, but I rammed into the bear with my shoulder in an attempt to push him back through the portal. Of course, nothing happened as he was roughly four times my size. The wolves began to circle back around to us, snarling.

"Move!" I yelled. He blinked at me, then turned and tumbled backward, disappearing into thin air. I ran after him, praying that whatever magic was at work here, the wolves would be unable to follow us.

The smell of roses washed over me again and I stood back in the garden, the stone castle basking in the afternoon sun.

The bear was nowhere to be seen. Instead the tall, dark, and scraggly mountain man stood in front of me, swaying on his feet. Blood dripped from his arm and soaked through the shoulder of his dark shirt. I suppose in a world with magic portals and talking forest creatures I shouldn't be surprised, but…

"You're the bear."

He nodded, and what I could see of his face between the hair and the beard seemed pale under the scars.

"And when you told me to wait until sunrise, you didn't mean that sun, did you?" I pointed up at the cheery midday sun.

"I did not."

"Okay, two more questions for you." I took a deep breath. This was clearly crazy. "Where am I? And are you going to pass out on me?"

"This is Kilinaire Castle," he replied. "You're in *Tír na nÓg*."

"Tirna-what-now?"

"Faerie," he said. "You're in Faerie. As for your second question, I hope not. But can we please go back inside now? I believe all the medical supplies are still laid out in the parlor." He touched his injured shoulder gingerly.

"Alright, Bear." I motioned for him to lead the way. "Back to the castle we go. But no fainting on me. You'd squash me like a bug."

Want to read the whole story? The Rose Gate, a Retelling of Beauty and the Beast *is available now!***

About the Author

H anna Sandvig is turning your favorite fairy tales into faerie tales with some sweet romance and enough sass to keep things interesting.

Hanna is living out her personal happily-ever-after in the mountains of BC, Canada with her husband, three little girls, and giant cat. When she's not writing, drawing, or reading, she can be found sewing, taking photos, baking, and desperately trying to not pick up any more creative pursuits. If you drop in to visit, please bring plenty of chocolate and strong black tea.